THE

EARTH

DOES NOT

GET

FAT

Praise for Julia Prendergast

Julia Prendergast is a real writer who writes about real life. There was a time when real life was to be sneered at, undeserving of an artist's attention. Fortunately life keeps insisting on our regard and Prendergast gives it that. She will be in the top echelon of Australian writers.

Bruce Pascoe

Julia Prendergast handles her themes – love and loss, independence and responsibility, fact and fantasy – with considerable skill. The darkness of her subject-matter is offset by the vigour of the language, the flashes of humour and the unmistakable compassion that underpins the narrative as a whole. An impressive debut.

Jem Poster

Julia lives in Melbourne with her circus of a family.

Julia's short stories have been longlisted, shortlisted and published: Lightship Anthology International Short Story Competition (UK), Ink Tears International Short Story Competition (UK), Glimmer Train International Short Story Competition (US), Séan Ó Faoláin International Short Story Competition (IE), *TEXT* (AU), *Review of Australian Fiction*, Australian Book Review Elizabeth Jolley Prize, Josephine Ulrick Prize (AU).

THE EARTH DOES NOT GET FAT

JULIA PRENDERGAST

UWA PUBLISHING

First published in 2018 by
UWA Publishing
Crawley, Western Australia 6009
www.uwap.uwa.edu.au

UWAP is an imprint of UWA Publishing,
a division of The University of Western Australia.

 A catalogue record for this
book is available from the
National Library of Australia

Cover design by Alissa Dinallo
Typeset in 11 pt Bembo by Lasertype
Printed by McPhersons Printing Group

This project has been assisted by the Australian Government
through the Australia Council, its arts funding and advisory body.

 uwapublishing

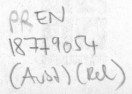

For Matthew
For our children—
Albert, Amelia, Grace, Henry, Matilda and Heidi

'The earth does not get fat', Nguni saying: however many dead it receives the earth is never satiated.

'Proverbs in Africa',
The Wisdom of Many. Essays on the Proverb, R. Finnegan

Mum, poor girl. She taught us compassion. She made us grow up quickly. And made us able to take on the world.

The Fighter, A. Zable

Contents

Chapter One

Colour me grey

Shades of grey:
The possibility of uncertainty

Cambridge Dictionary

Sometimes Mum's already sinking when I get home from school. She takes more pills, washes them down with a few slugs of gin on ice, just a dash of tonic, and finally she's out, flat out, on the couch. After a few hours pass, I know she's down for good.

Getting her into bed is the hardest part because I can't carry her on my own. She doesn't weigh much, but it's awkward and so I put a blanket on the floor next to the couch and I move her onto that. I reach under her shoulders and move her top half down first. Sometimes her head bangs on the floorboards because I can't hold it properly. Sometimes she opens one eye, just for a second. Still she can't see me for the grey.

I pull the rest of her onto the blanket. Her legs thud against the floorboards like old potatoes; she doesn't flinch.

I drag her across the floor, pulling her along on the blanket. The floor in the bedroom is carpeted so the last stretch is ugly, her head to one side, nodding awkwardly against the taut blanket, mouth open. Before I try to lift her, I lay some old towels down, in case she wets the bed.

If Grandad is in a decent mood, he helps me. We usually get Mum in after a few attempts. I tuck her legs under the covers and wipe her sweaty face on my sleeve. If her skin feels like cold lasagne, I use a warm cloth to revive her face. If Grandad's being difficult she has to stay there on the floor. I put some pillows and a doona down there to soften things up, but still, she's left on the floor like nobody cares.

She stays in the shadowy place for a couple of days, waking briefly to top herself up. She has a pen beside her bed and she marks lines on the paper, keeping tabs of her intake. The scribble looks like a hangman scoresheet.

We've lived with Grandad since I was a baby. He's all that's left of Mum's family. In the beginning his mind was intact. Even now, he can sense when Mum is in trouble. He gets busy in his room. He tries to fix something: a broken chair leg, the handle of a pot, anything. I hear him humming. He always hums when he's engrossed in something: classical-sounding tunes, no lyrics. I ask him, again and again, if he wants to listen to music, but he says: No, no, I like the quiet, and then he starts humming again. He reacts to Mum's greyness in his way even though his mind is half gone. I suppose you never get used to seeing someone you love all fucked up like that.

After we've put Mum to bed and Grandad is pottering away in his room, I make a start on dinner. I'm standing over the boiling pasta when I hear Grandad say my name.

I turn to him and he has shit all over his hands. At first I think he's been into the bolognese sauce, but that's only because I'm exhausted and I can't see straight. He looks at his shitty hands as if he's not sure what it is. Then he holds his palms out to me like he's begging.

I yell at him not to touch anything. I take him to the bathroom and wash his hands and fingernails, four times with the scrubbing brush. I tell him to lean on me and I help him step out of his pants. His droopy, shit-smeared balls jangle around because he can't balance properly.

Those undies are going straight in the bin, I say, talking to myself, reassuring myself that I won't need to scrub that thick adult shit off his pants.

They're my favourite ones, he says, please Chelsea, don't throw them in the bin. They're not itchy and they don't dig in. He is crying. His upper chest is heaving out like a pregnant woman's belly, dipping hollow between his ribcage so that he looks like a mangy bird, sick and pathetic.

I tell him: I'll get you some new undies. Really comfy ones. I'll get you a whole new packet, all different colours. You can come with me and pick out the ones you want.

They're my favourite, he says, becoming hysterical.

Well, you shouldn't have shat in them. I am yelling, feeling suffocated by the steamy claustrophobia of the shit.

I didn't know it was coming, he says desperately. I was busy. I didn't realise it was coming.

Busy, I scoff, and then I think that I might vomit because I love him so much ... I remember that I must never forget.

No crying, I say. Please, Grand, no crying today. I get him into the shower and adjust the taps until he says it's just right. Then I go out to get a rubbish bag, knowing all the

3

while that I'll go to bed feeling guilty if I throw out his favourite undies, knowing all the while that I'll be up to my elbows in old man's shit any minute.

I give him intimate instructions about how to wash himself. I show him again how to lather the soap in his hands. I bend over and mime it for him, rubbing all around. Then do it again, I say, lift up your balls, get right into all the creases and cracks.

Each day I have to remind him about basic stuff and he's not even that old. I didn't know you could get dementia before you were really old.

When Grandad is on the third round of lathering and rubbing, I close the shower screen and coach him from the outside. I take the filthy undies to the toilet and turn them inside out, hoping the shit will drop out in one lump. The stubborn foulness holds fast. I go back to the bathroom, using my hands and then the nailbrush, I work furiously at the basin. When I've finally finished, rinsed and disinfected, I open the shower door.

Time to get out, I say. Grandad is sitting at the base of the shower, shaving his legs. He has cut himself along the shin and the creamy tiles are covered in bloody water.

Don't move, I say, taking the razor. Sit there and *do not move*. I rush to the kitchen and grab some bandaids and a tea towel. When I come back, he is sitting right where I left him and I take a good look at the cut. *Fuck!* I say.

I beg your pardon, he says and that makes me laugh because he doesn't make the connection between my swearing and his bleeding leg. He has no idea. He's not even looking at me. He is intent on the blood, but he's detached from it, too——might as well be talking to the telly.

4

I start crying quietly then because the poor old bastard wouldn't hurt a fly. He looks up at me and his torso disappears. His head looks as though it's propped on his knees, long arms on either side like an albino monkey.

Never mind, he says. Everything will be fine. Just you wait and see. He turns back to his leg. He runs his fingers up his shin, inspecting the watery blood.

I take a roll of toilet paper from the bathroom drawer. Grandad holds the toilet paper against his shin and I dry his body. He bends forward and applies pressure to his leg.

It is pathetic. He is pathetic. I am pathetic. I should be handling it better. I'm not even done here and already the motherfucking guilt.

I dry him gently in long, deliberate strokes, along his back, across his shoulders. His veins are thick and strong and so exposed. His skin is wet and thin, like damp tissue paper. He looks older, with his wet skin and his wet hair, slick and silvery black against his bony skull. He looks old enough to have dementia.

He bends forward, holding his leg, trying to be helpful and obedient; his wrinkly old balls sag between his legs. He is helpless and endearing and revolting, like an old, ugly baby, and now I understand how mothers can love ugly babies, even when they're crying and covered in vomit and shit. It's because of the need. Need is very seductive.

I don't miss one drop. I dry him gently and firmly, behind his ears, inside his ears, under his armpits, behind his knees. I do it on auto because I know his body like my own. I put bandaids over the cut and wrap the tea towel tightly around his shin to keep up the pressure. Then I roll some deodorant under his armpits and he laughs. He says it tickles. Do it again, he begs.

I give him a squirt of my body spray. Ooh that's lovely, he says. I kiss him on the forehead and hold out his pyjamas so he can step into them. Then I blow the dryer over his hair and brush it away from his face.

I throw his clothes in the washing machine: hot water, double powder, pre-wash and soak. I stand still, my hands against the warm lid of the machine, listening to the swish of the water, mesmerised. It's like the waves are lapping the shore, right at my feet, as if I don't have a care in the world, as if I have nothing better to do than stand in the sun and watch the water.

Grandad comes to the laundry and stands beside me, his hand on the machine beside mine. You are a very lucky girl, he says. Do you know how lucky you are?

I don't answer him. I put my hand on his. I'm waiting for the hidden camera crew to reveal themselves, then we can all have a laugh, we can all say: Of course that's not her real life. It's a joke. We stand beside the washing machine a few more moments, still and content, as if life's a holiday.

Grandad kisses me softly on the cheek and then wanders off to his room. I go to the kitchen to see if I can salvage the pasta. I dish it all up and put a bowl of shredded cheese beside Grandad's plate. He likes to add that by himself and I'm not up for another meltdown.

I knock on his door and step into his room. He is already asleep. My school shoes are placed neatly beside his bed. He has polished them until they look like new, and they were nearly ready for the bin.

When Mum is stuck in the grey, Grandad often goes for the shoes, scrubbing the soles and wiping the surfaces with a hot cloth. He places a few drops of eucalyptus oil inside them, polishing them up until they're so shiny, you'd think we were in the army. It's a bit of a wasted effort on his part, because I don't worry too much about school these days.

I say: I am a very lucky girl. I'm crying hard and kissing him. I say: I know how lucky I am. He doesn't flinch, just sighs contentedly in his sleep. I know he can hear me. People can hear you in their sleep. I talk to Mum all the time. I tell her all the things I can't say when she's awake, staring at me with her eyes full of grey.

I go back to the kitchen and pour myself a gin and tonic, a double. I decide to have Grandad's undies fresh and ready for him when he wakes in the morning.

Everything will be fine, I say. Just you wait and see.

Chapter Two

Sundowning

Sundowning: also known as Sundown Syndrome, a term
used to refer to [behavioural] changes that often occur in
the late afternoon or evening in people with Alzheimer's
disease and similar conditions. The [behavioural]
changes ... take the form of aggression, agitation,
delusions, hallucinations, paranoia, increased disorientation,
or wandering and pacing about

MedicineNet.com

I'm up at five am because Grandad thinks it's dinnertime.
He's sundowning and it's not even daylight. I'm cooking
pasta and heating up bolognese sauce by five-thirty. I have
extra meals plated and the dishes done by six-fifteen. By
eight-fifteen Grandad is asleep on the couch and I decide to
head into school for a few hours, see how much I've missed,
see if it's still within my reach.

I sit up the back with Tiff and Jules. Andy and Dom are
there because they don't let Tiff out of their sight. Andy has
a goon bag in his big black pencil case. He has it zipped up,
just the tap poking out, and they're sucking back the dry
white wine, pretending to get busy with their pens if Ms
Luscombe looks our way.

Andy passes the goon along to me. His pencil case is
bursting like a fat black seal. I stand my binder book up

on the desk and have a good long swig. I've been up half the night, so it feels like the afternoon to me. I've been sundowning since sunrise.

Ms Luzzy is called out to attend to something or other because she's the Year Twelve coordinator as well as our English teacher. We're in that class because we're capable workers, the top of the barrel, the pick of the crop, and she reminds us of this, and of the great and glorious things expected of us, and then she leaves, itching her thigh through her scratchy, grey woollen skirt, her doughnut ankles spewing out of her worn, black square-heeled shoes.

Dom lights a fag, right there on the floor in the corner of the classroom, and I can't resist a drag. He smells like soap and aftershave and I want to undo his shirt, lay my head on his chest and blow smoke up at the roof as if we've just rooted each other senseless. Dom has kind blue eyes and he smiles at me like he knows what I'm up against. His eyes sparkle as if he wants to root me senseless, too.

I light a fag of my own and blow smoke at Dom's face. His eyes glaze over and he's grinning. It looks like he's doing some sundowning of his own. Sundowning isn't reserved for the twilight hours. You can sundown any time of the day. It's the tiredness that makes things blur and shift, and I'm always tired because Grandad and Mum turn night into day, day into night.

I have a great long drag until the tip is dark brown and wrong, but God it tastes good. I blow smoke down at the floor because I can't even look at Dom and I guzzle the wine.

By the time Luzzy gets back I'm sorted. I'm well on my way to a smashing introduction of my *Pride and Prejudice* text response. I focus specifically on Mrs Bennet, thinking

I'll throw Nelly in from *Wuthering Heights*. I'll talk about underhanded and overhanded manipulation, the criss-crossed blurring of the two. Everything is crisscrossed and blurry when you're as tired as I am, but things are clearer than ever, too, crystal sundowning clear.

I decide I'll get the essay organised and head home early. I want to check on Grandad. All this talk of books, with the taste of wine on my tongue, it makes me dream of a long, hot bath—nothing quite like it, a fag, a glass of wine and a good book in the bath.

I'll open the window and let the fresh air in. I'll have the bath so hot I can hardly bear it and then everything will be as clear as a bell. I'll be able to hear Mrs Bennet and I'll feel Nelly lurking like a shadow in the hallway. They're sundowners from way back, those two, underhanded and overhanded line-blurrers, the both of them.

I'll see you after class, Chelsea, says Luzzy Lezzy. I'm lost in my thoughts and she comes as a shock. Why does she have to announce it like that? I *will* see you. No please may I? No are you available? She's as rude as her ankles.

Andy and Dom are giggling and snorting and Luzzy says: Perhaps you'd like to see me at lunchtime, boys? She raises a pubey eyebrow and that shuts them up.

Everyone spills out into the hallway. Dom is the last out the door and he gives me a wink. Ms Luscombe launches straight in: It's not good enough, Chelsea. Your results aren't enough. Not on their own. You must attend classes or you'll fail.

I roll my eyes at her because she's a total fuck-knuckle. She probably memorises those lines in bed at night, going over the words in her head, all prudied up in her old-lady pyjamas.

Her husband would be next to her, fidgeting, desperate for a root, but she wouldn't even notice.

Luzzy says: I'm going to have to call your parents. It's protocol. I'll schedule a meeting with your mum and dad to discuss your future at the college.

She says 'college' to make it sound like more than it is. It's a Catholic co-ed nothing. I have no idea why Mum sent me here. It's so yesterday.

Luzzy stares at me hard, the pores of her skin open and exposed, like moon craters. Her small pupils widen. I've never been this close. She says: Well, Chelsea? Her breath is stale, not necessarily bad, but certainly not fresh. What have you got to say for yourself?

Whatever, I say.

It is not *whatever*, she spits, talking through her teeth. This is *your* future. You're cheating yourself, miss. She says 'Miss' angrily, hissing it out like she wants to say 'bitch', and she's only cheating herself because I couldn't give a shit what she calls me and she's just missing the rush and the release of letting it out.

She says: Have you been drinking? I can smell alcohol and cigarettes. I have a nose for it.

She moves in so close that we're inhaling each other's breath. Chelsea, do you have a substance-abuse problem?

I'm still looking at her nose and I'm thinking that her husband probably can't get it up and that's why she's so frustrated.

I'm speaking to you, Chelsea. You will do me the courtesy …

Someone should do you the courtesy, do you hard and fast from behind. Then you mightn't be so uptight.

Luzzy says: I'm waiting, Chelsea, because this isn't just about you. Do you *honestly* think you're being fair to your family?

Fuck off, I say, under my breath.

I beg your pardon.

Go and fuck yourself, I say, loud and clear.

Later that day, Luzzy calls my house. She sounds even more frustrated on the phone.

She says: Hello, this is Christine Luscombe. May I speak to Anne Withers?

I say: Speaking. I'm onto my second glass of wine, my second load of washing and ironing. I'm feeling calm, on top of things.

Hello, Mrs Withers.

Call me Anne, I say, taking a long sip of the woody white wine.

Anne. I'm calling to talk to you about Chelsea's frequent absences from school and to discuss an unfortunate misdemeanour today—

I interrupt: Yes, Chelsea told me about today. She was very upset. Luzzy stays quiet so I take the lead. The thing is, Chelsea's grandfather lives with us and he requires full-time care. He suffers from dementia.

Oh.

I'm not always in a position to provide that care, Ms Luscombe.

Call me Christine.

Christine. I cannot always care for Chelsea's grandfather because I suffer from rheumatoid arthritis, utterly debilitating. Some days I can't turn on a tap, some days I can barely get out of bed.

Oh. That's awful.

Chelsea is a private kid, holds her cards close. She wouldn't want the other students to know what she's contending with at home, but the reality is that Chelsea is the full-time carer.

Oh, if only we'd known. Oh, Anne, I'm so sorry.

Call me Annie, I say, taking another sip.

Annie. We can fill in some forms so that Chelsea won't be penalised for her sporadic attendance. Also, she should qualify for special consideration if we document the situation properly. Could you come in, fill in some forms?

I say: It'd be best if you would post them or send them home with Chelsea. I'm not great at the moment and Chelsea's grandfather has had pneumonia, on top of everything else. That's why she flew off the handle today. She's very embarrassed that she lashed out, swearing at you like she did.

Well, it makes sense now, in light of …

Poor kid, she only had a few hours' sleep last night, between me and her grandfather.

If only I'd known, she says. I'll need to meet with Chelsea on Monday because I've documented it, you see, it's on the record, although I'm sure we can move on quickly. I'd like to clear the air with her—of course there'll be no repercussions. We'll have a chat; I'll just table it with her briefly. I'll get hold of the documents this afternoon and set things in motion for the special consideration. Thank you, Annie. Thanks.

No. Thank you, Christine. Please, if you could keep this under your hat, because Chelsea's a private kid.

Of course …

I hang up the phone, feeling pretty pleased with myself. Rheumatoid arthritis, it's supposed to be a bastard of a thing.

Mum is asleep and Grandad is settled in front of the telly. I open the window to let the fresh air in because I don't want him falling asleep. Only two hours until I can put him to bed for the night. I take another load of washing out to the line. I'm beyond tired, too tired to sleep, past the point.

As I hang the last shirt I can hear Grandad yelling. I run inside. It's a quick turn and that's a bad sign. The yelling is coming from Mum's room.

Annie, you wake up now. You wake up *right now* ... You're *not* dead; you're *not* dead. Wake up. *Wake up!*

When I get to Mum's bedroom, Grandad is standing over her with his fists clenched. He has tears and snot running down his cheeks and chin, and blood on his fists. He wipes it on his face. The blood is from Mum; her nose is bleeding and there is blood at the corner of her mouth. Her cheeks and eyes are shiny, rosy red from the punches.

Grandad is moaning through his teeth. It's a mixture of breathing and moaning. He sounds like an injured animal, like he's possessed.

Stop it! I yell. *Stop it right now.* I grab his arm. She's not dead, I say. She's asleep.

She won't wake up. She doesn't wake up.

She's sick, I say. That's why she can't wake up. *Because she's sick.* I am slurring and crying and doing the possessed breathing too. The sickness makes her sleep hard and deep. She can't help it.

14

I put my arm around Grandad and steer him out of the bedroom. I look down at the grass-green carpet and I know there's nothing more hopeless than green carpet.

Before I know it, I have Luzzy at my door. I've had time to collect myself, but it knocks me—she's ambushing me, arriving at my home unannounced.

I thought I'd drop over the special-consideration forms, she says. Did your mum tell you about it? She looks over my shoulder, trying to get a glimpse of the inside. This is after school, twilight, official sundowning time.

I move closer to the doorway and pull the door, holding it behind my back. I am squeezed between the door and the outside world. Luzzy can't see a thing. How dare she arrive at my doorstep, at my home? She has no fucking right.

Luzzy says: We need to keep you at school, Chelsea. It would be such a waste if you dropped out. You have a fine mind. You're the cream of the crop.

Whatever, I say.

She sighs. It is not *whatever*. You don't know what you're saying. You have no idea how important this is.

Grandad comes up behind me, holding his bowl out in front of him. He is dressed in his saggy undies and a singlet. He has bolognese sauce all around his mouth, down his front. He says: Can I have some more please, Shells?

I turn to Luzzy and I say: Look, I need to get back to it so … I try to close the door.

Luzzy puts her hand in the way. She says: Can I have a word to Annie?

No! … No, you can't.

15

Why not?

She's unavailable.

I'd really like to speak to Annie, says Luzzy.

Annie is sick, says Grandad. That's why she can't wake up. She's not *dead*, she's sick. I thought she was dead. That's why I punched her. It was only an accident.

Luzzy looks at me for an explanation. Is it true? she asks. Did he punch her?

He's sundowning, I say. It's true to him.

He's *what?*

Look it up in the dictionary, I say, flicking her hand away and closing the door firmly.

Chapter Three

Sawdust

Crossword clues for 'Powdery wood particles'

Clue	Answer
Powdery wood particles (7)	Sawdust
Small wood particles (7)	Sawdust
Powdered wood (7)	Sawdust
Particles of cut wood (7)	Sawdust

http://www.the-crossword-solver.com/word/powdery+wood+particles

I wake to the sound of a chainsaw and yelling. When I look out of the window I see the tree-men on the ground, yelling fucken this and fucken that, calling to the young man, perched halfway up the grey-white gum.

I can't believe they are taking down the tree. I know it looks a bit dangerous, leaning out over the road, but they don't have to get rid of it. It's my favourite tree. I watch it when Melbourne flips from sunny calm to angry windstorm. I watch it in the wind before the rain, the tangle before the wash. The silvery, spear-shaped leaves gust up, up, like a madwoman's hair, and it reminds me that even in nature, one thing is another.

The tree-man climbs the smooth grey trunk as if he is a spider. The spikes in his shoes hack into the tree, his footsteps biting angrily into the grey sheen of the trunk.

The marks are sharp and definite, like a seagull's feet on wet sand.

God, I miss the water. I miss walking along the beach with the wind in my face. The waves make me feel new as they wash my old footprints away. Even in this black-rock, industrial, seaside nothing, I can pretend I am somewhere else when I have the wind in my face and the wash on my feet.

Grey-white gums are shaped like skinny, strong men—muscle and bone, nothing else. The young man is stringy and tough like the tree. He places the rope around the upper branches as if he is brushing long hair away from his lover's face. He digs his feet into the trunk, rooting himself in place. His arms are busy with the rope; he is engrossed by it, precise about it. He is gentle and efficient, his torso shifting, writhing with the movements of his arms.

I ring Ellen from next door. I ask her if I can have the wood. She says: The men will leave the wood on the nature strip—of course you're welcome to it, darling.

I go out the front and approach the two men on the ground. They are holding the rope that is attached to the tree's branches. I wait for the chainsaw to idle. I watch the younger man in the tree as he lowers the chainsaw. He drops it first, just below his spiked feet and then he shakes the rope, lowering it further still. He does this seamlessly, effortlessly, as if he is shaking a tambourine against his thigh, dancing a little. The chainsaw hangs above us, whirring evenly like an electric knife.

The tree-man's torso is like a board, a concrete slab, a block that turns with the movements of his arms and legs. The power is all his and we are all aware of this as we stare up at him, mesmerised, silvery sawdust raining down.

Hi, I say, turning back to the men on the ground, my face flushed.

Morning, says one of the men. The other man grunts, eyes skyward, clutching the rope as if his life depends on it.

I just talked to Ellen, the woman inside, I say, pointing towards the front door. She said I could take the wood.

He smirks: You?

Yes, I say. I know I'm on the skinny side, but I'm strong. He knows nothing about me. How dare he question what I am capable of? I stare back, hard: If someone stops off to ask, can you say it's taken?

Yeah alright, and I'll tell him, he says, pointing to the tree-man. He'll be doing the clean-up.

Thanks, I say, glancing up the tree again, before going inside.

By the time I've hung out a second load of washing, the gum is level with the pitch of the roof. Ghostly, ghostly gum. Turning silver-white at night, turning branches into gnarled arms and rustling to whispers. I watch the disappearance of the grey-white trunk. I watch it felled, mourn it fallen, and I realise that although it may be gone, somehow it's still there.

The tree-man stands astride the trunk, unclipping the buckle at his belt, loosening the rope so that he can manoeuvre the chainsaw more freely. He straddles the trunk then, until he's almost flat against it, and he cuts into it on an angle. With his feet so firmly rooted into the body of the tree, he seems to float on air.

After cutting a large wedge from both sides of the trunk, the tree-man re-clips the chainsaw to his flank. He whacks the top piece of the trunk, thwacks it with the flat of his palms, encouraging it to fall in precisely the way that he would like it to fall.

I get stuck into the housework. Everything will be okay, I tell myself, and I believe it. I'm feeling good, excited about the wood. I've been rationing the last of the woodpile, trying not to use it all. The good wood, the slow-burning stuff, is hard to come by.

When I'm through with all of the regular washing and I'm onto the bedsheets, I hear the sound of a garden blower. I peer through the window; the clean-up is underway. The men throw all the smaller, twiggy branches onto the back of the truck and shred them to mulch. Only the logs are left.

As the truck pulls away, the older man winds down the window. He waves to the tree-man and calls: Don't work too hard, laughing through grey-brown teeth. The tree-man waves them away with his free arm. I approach him, feeling awkward, hoping the other men told him I was coming.

It's the way he took the tree down that makes me nervous, as if he knew its nooks and crevices, as if he had spent his entire life staring at that tree. I'm not sure what to expect of him, now that he is back on the ground. When I get within a few paces, he flicks the blower switch over to idle and pushes the earmuffs down around his neck. His face is wet, dripping with sweat.

I put the wheelbarrow down. I'm taking the wood, I say and he nods and smiles. His eyes are blue and I am surprised. His hair and beard are dark and I imagined that his eyes would be dark, too. It's as though he has someone else's eyes.

I turn away, picking up the closest log and heaving it into the wheelbarrow. Gum is such heavy wood, dense like concrete, and because the tree was in its prime, the wood is wet, weighty with life. One log is as much as I will be able to carry. I wheel it along the footpath and then into our driveway. If I can just get the wood into our front yard, I'll be happy with that. It doesn't matter if it takes me the rest of the year to get it around the back.

The job is much harder than I imagined. The fronts of my thighs are aching. My shoulders and arms are burning. I have lugged wood before, but the dead weight of the gum is overwhelming. As I begin the third run, I am breathless and sweaty and I consider packing it in.

The tree-man is loading the blower into the back of the ute. As I get close, he takes the wheelbarrow, gliding up Ellen's driveway as if he were riding a scooter, continuing in the way that I have started, except with such ease. I am too spent to argue and there's nothing to argue with anyway, nothing verbal.

Generally, I'm reluctant to accept help. I'd prefer to do the job myself, so I don't owe anyone. Today, I can't do it alone. I peel off my cardigan, wiping the sweat from under my eyes, between my breasts. I wrap the cardie around my hips and take a few deep breaths.

I lift the big logs with the tree-man. I don't even know if they could be described as logs, those larger pieces of the trunk. He wheels them away and I follow him, carrying a smaller log or two by hand. These I won't need to split, they're the perfect width to go over the kindling, just as they are.

When I've carried as much as I can, I clutch his forearm and say: Enough. That's enough. I'm still puffing and he did most of the work. No wonder his torso is a rock. I put my elbows on my knees and bend over, holding my head in my hands, catching my breath. When I straighten up, he is brushing the sawdust from his jumper—with the glint of sunshine across his shoulder it looks like papery glitter.

You want a drink? I ask.

He nods. I take my shoes off at the door and he does the same, placing them neatly before he comes inside. On the way to the kitchen, I close Mum's bedroom door. I am careful to be quiet, even though there's no need. She's out for it, day three, comatose, fuck-eyed—if you lift the eyelid that's what you'll see: the elsewhere eyes of a dead person.

I wonder what the tree-man would think if he went in to Mum—mottled sheets, piss and bile, the giddy-green carpet. Sawdust mother …

I pull a stool out from the kitchen bench and he sits. Grandad is asleep on the couch and I turn up the television so that our talk won't disturb him.

My grandad, I say to the tree-man. He's asleep.

He nods.

He has dementia, I add.

I reach into the fridge for the water jug, but I spy the soda water so I grab that instead. I take two glasses from the cupboard and half fill them with ice. I put the icetray back in the freezer and grab the vodka, pouring it over the ice, a good whack of it. I hold up the bottle, glancing at the tree-man, reassuring myself that he's not a dream. He nods, the quiver of a smile at his lips. Mostly, he smiles with his eyes. The silence is not uncomfortable: it's quite cosy but charged, fully charged.

I add a dash of lime cordial and take a small sip. I like to taste the vodka and the lime, bang on, before I add the fizz.

I add the soda and whisk the glasses with a fork. I down it. The tree-man does the same.

I add more ice and make another round. We drink the second one just as quickly. Why not? I mix a third. I take the glasses and walk towards the hallway, nodding at him to follow. I am beginning to get nervous that we'll wake Grandad and I'm not ready to let the tree-man go, not yet. As we pass the bathroom he detours and I wait for him.

When we get to my bedroom, I hand him a glass and turn on the light. I move the blankets from the chair in the corner of the room, laying them on the floor at the end of my bed. He doesn't sit.

He takes a long sip, draining the glass, and puts it on the chair. He waits for me to drink, and then he takes my glass and places it next to his. He sweeps the loose hair away from my face as if I am a ghostly gum, as if his hands know me better than I know myself. I kiss him, I know how to kiss. I can smell cut tree and his clean-sweat smell. I can taste the vodka, the bitter sweat on his neck. His jumper is tight. As he peels it off, I smell sweat and soap and aftershave, sweet and sour like yesterday. I can smell cut trees and felled ghosts. I imagined his torso as a block, a concrete coffin, but it is dark and matted like his beard, and so warm.

I kiss the tree-man, and he holds me with strong, gentle hands and invisible ropes, as if he knows where my body will give and fall. Before I realise that he has a hold, I am trembling beyond the beat, just outside time, breathless, like a tambourine.

When we are back in real time, I say: What's your name? He lifts his head, preparing to sit up, readying himself to answer me. I imagine that his voice is like his beard, dark, twisted.

Never mind, I say, kissing him softly and insistently so he can't answer. I prefer the sweaty tangle of the silence.

Chapter Four

Long gone

Long gone: having ended, died, disappeared

Merriam Webster Dictionary

Dear Chelsea,

I've been over it in my head so many times. Over and over. Now I'm writing it down.

I wonder if this is how things seemed to you, back then. I wonder if you remember it like this, now ... I wonder if you can forgive me.

We were different. Outsiders.

We stuck together. We were a bit left of centre, whatever that means.

Your mum didn't leave the house. She spent days in bed. Out of it.

In the beginning, you said: She's an enigma. Then you said: If you ask questions, I won't walk home with you. After that I just talked about random stuff and I didn't ask anything. I wanted to be near you, so I tried not to annoy you.

I wished my parents were enigmas. My mum was so in my face I could barely breathe my own breath. My parents are conservative Catholics, oldschool, like from the 1920s. They live in the long-gone—drinking and smoking are first-class misdemeanours. If they caught me with booze or smokes on my breath, I'd be in exile at Catholic-land, so I stayed pure.

They're still that way and I'm a uni student. It's so strange.

I'm not a smoker anyway so that was no big deal, but the grog I liked. I had a few beers one night at Steve's. Do you remember? The aftermath with my parents was unbearable: sin and darkness, betrayal of trust. They went crazy, as if I'd nailed Jesus to the cross myself: temptation and evil, getting caught up with the pack mentality. On and on.

At first I tried to be like you. I started swearing all the time. It sounded good when you swore so I tried to take some of it on, except it sounded too polite, almost apologetic. You giggled at me like I was a try-hard. You were right: I was trying too hard.

The only thing I couldn't bring myself to say was cunt. Uncle Archie's mate said it at Christmas and that spoiled things for everyone. This mate of Archie's (Ron) was over from Perth for a spell (his wife gave him the flick). Mum and Aunty Jean had just finished serving the sweaty turkey lunch and Archie was talking about summer holidays. Dad said that he couldn't get any holidays until we went back to school because senior management had blocked out all of January.

Ron said: Selfish cunts.

Mum lost it. She was hysterical. She was so cut up about it that we had to leave. We were all starving. I had the turkey on my fork. She didn't care. Dad bought us McDonald's on the way home. Mum didn't even argue and she hates Maccas. We ate our lunch in a park across the road. It was actually more like an easement. Dodgy as. Mum ate her fillet-o-fish between stabs of crying and deep sighs. Dad said: It's okay … it's okay, as if he felt sorry for her. He has a vein on his left eyebrow that throbs when he's angry and it was pumping.

The plum pudding, said Mum, we won't even get to taste it. I took a lot of time, soaking the fruit in brandy: it was V.S.O.P. It even has fresh dates in it. It'll be the best one ever. Could you …?

Could I *what?* By now Dad was as close to yelling as he ever came. It's Christmas Day, not a glass of wine in sight. We're eating … McDonald's in a vacant park for … sake.

He was desperate to swear. He was spitting out his words, staggering over them and spraying pieces of big mac over the grass. I knew that he wasn't saying everything he wanted to say because I could hear the words … in waiting. I could hear them lilting in the silence between those he spoke.

Lilting … I know about it from playing the guitar. It's supposed to be about the rise and fall of the chords, or the voice. For me it's only ever about the falling. It's meant to be a tripping rhythm, like a missing beat—really it's a shadow, a falling shadow. Falling not fallen. Long gone but so there.

I'm not going back to get the … pudding, said Dad, and that's that.

You taught me that words aren't harmful on their own. It depends how they're said, what is meant. When you swore, I was thinking about why. I was thinking of the words around the word. I was thinking context and intent. In Mum's case, the word was a stopping point she couldn't get past.

When I went to parties, Dom and the other guys would rag on me because I didn't get pissed. You said: Don't worry, Geoff. Those mainstream cunts wouldn't know their arse from their elbow. It's my favourite thing you ever said. I sucked the air in through my teeth because I was shocked, hearing you say it. At the same time, I was totally chuffed because you'd put us in the same boat, downstream from mainstream.

My parents always picked me up at midnight: that was my curfew. Otherwise, they were too tired for mass in the morning. If things got messy, I waited out the front. I didn't want Mum to see everyone, passing over today and into the long-gone. At the very least, I tried to be right near the door when she arrived. Mum always stepped inside if she could. She waltzed in like Jesus on water, as if it was her God-given right to meddle in every corner of my life.

You told me I should pop a pill or something. You said my parents wouldn't smell a pill on your breath: I'd be filled with the love of Christ and they'd be over the moon.

You twisted your long, shiny hair around your finger. You said: See what it feels like to be the messiah for a night; see what all the fuss is about. Everything's a fucken miracle. Try it. You threw your head back and laughed. It was sickeningly seductive. You knew it was. You must have known.

I didn't laugh. I didn't think it was such a cracking idea. You wanted me to let my hair down and I wanted to loosen up, but I was nervous. I wanted you too much and it made me careful. When your mum was good, you let your hair down. I'm making the most of it, you said.

Who can tell if you've ever really made the most of anything? Is your best the most? Sometimes my best is weak as. Sometimes the most is broken, hollow.

My mum is strange and I worry that I'm strange, too, and it makes me strange, worrying about it, second-guessing my every move until I've missed all my chances and I'm lilting in the long-gone. When I was with you, I forgot about Mum and it made me less strange. It unstranged me.

At Steve's, I forgot about Mum so much that I wasn't waiting near the door. The music was loud and I was lilting in it. I was watching the toilet door for you, guarding it, making sure no one barged in. You looked pale, like you might throw.

When I heard Mum's voice, I went out to the living room. Dom was standing there with his arm around Mum's shoulders. He had a vodka bottle full of water in his hand and he was off his head. He stepped back from Mum, holding the bottle out to her, slurring. He said: How 'bout you do the water-into-wine trick? He was wobbling all over the place, laughing. Mum was standing stiff and straight like a goalpost. It was awful.

I was angry with Mum because she weaselled in and brought it on herself, but I was dark with all of the others, too, for standing around and laughing in a pack, with a pack mentality. Mum's God-loving is obsessive, even deranged, although she would never be mean to anyone, not intentionally. It's a sickening thing, having your mum right in the thick of funny.

Dom was losing his footing with the force of his laughter. Mum's face was deadpan, dead as a pan. Dom leered at her, swaying. He said: C'mon, Mrs Musgrove. Show us a bit of the talking in tongues, then? He lobbed his tongue out, flicking it around his lips, making a noise that sounded like a wounded yodel, cut up by his laughing. He was waving his arms around as if he was dancing, although his legs were still.

Mum stood rigid, always and ever the post, pale and wide-eyed.

Enough! I said, turning Mum towards the door. Everyone froze. Someone stopped the music and everything was quiet. I led Mum out, taking her by the arm as if she was blind.

And the blind shall see and the deaf shall hear. Even the stuff that's long gone: over and done.

I looked back when I got to the door, remembering you. You stared at me, confused, one hand against the wall to steady yourself.

As we backed out of the driveway, I saw you standing near the lounge-room window. You pulled the curtain aside. Dom came up behind you: spiky hair, broad shoulders. He edged his face closer to your neck.

My mum goes to prayer group with Dom's mum and I figure she has her fair share to pray about, having a cunt for a son.

Arriving at school the following Monday, I was nervous, thinking everyone would be talking about the Mum-Show, but that was old news. Everyone was talking about you and Dom. Suddenly, I wished they were talking about Mum. I felt sick with the visuals. Ben walked in on you and you were both starkers, up to your ears in it, apparently.

I was fantasising all kinds of rampant bestial sex, you and Dom, all the positions, all the possibilities. Then I overheard Tiff say that your mum was down the gurgler and that's why you weren't at school. Just like that, my disgust was long gone. I wanted to help you. I wanted to tell you I'd always be there. I wanted to say you could hook up with anyone you wanted, including me of course.

When your mum was bad you didn't leave the house. It was like hibernating and there were no in-betweens. It was all or nothing, on or off, and I tried to understand the pressure. I hoped that's why you went for Dom and I pretended it meant nothing. I tried not to do my head in about it because you might have been doing other stuff, not the deed, and I tried not to worry if you did or you didn't because it was over and done and one day it would be long gone.

I didn't see you for ages after that and I was beginning to feel like you were the enigma. I turned up to the parties, just in case, but I left quietly when you weren't there. By the time summer rolled around, I'd just about given up. Tiff's party was a last-ditch attempt.

We sat around the back garden breathing the jasmine-scented air, punchbowl in the middle of the table, cicadas going crazy. I filled my plastic cup with Tiff's punch, loads of pineapple juice and crushed ice, shitloads of vodka. I eyeballed you so that you'd know I was alive, ready to let my hair down. It was a balmy night and everyone was looking bronze and chilled out from the summer holidays, except for you. You looked strung out and skinny.

When you got up from the table, I took a breath or two; that's as long as I could wait, and then I followed. I stepped out through the front door and saw you heading down the driveway.

Wait, I said. I'll walk you home.

I'll be fine, you said.

Please, I said. Let me walk you.

Do you remember me pleading? I was so … desperate for you.

We walked fast, mostly in silence. I reached down and held your hand. You looked at me sideways, but then you held on tight and we marched on. When we got to your place you walked up the concrete steps to the front door and turned around, still puffing. I stood on the ground below, looking up at you as if I was begging, praying. You lit a smoke and sucked it hard. Your blue eyes turned black as you narrowed them, scrutinising me.

You looked a bit mean sometimes. Maybe not mean, just hard. You were beautiful, don't get me wrong, utterly stunning. You smoked like an old-timer, blowing it out soft and long, lips pursed, and then a couple of rings at the end, just for kicks. I hate smoking, cigarettes sicken me, only with you, like the swearing, there was something seductive about it. I could watch you swear and smoke all day long.

Thanks for walking me, you said.

It's a fair way, I said. I can't believe you walk that by yourself, at night.

I run, you said.

I thought about how you lived on the other side of town, the industrial quarter, while most of us lived on the school side, the trendy side. Some people say the sea is different on the wrong side of town. Smelly. It's the same sea of course, just two kilometres south, but on the dodgy side they say the sea is dirty and depressing, smarmy and oily, slick with working-people's filth. It's an awful thing to say.

I stood there, looking up at you, inhaling deeply through my nose: trying to smell it. You stared at me suspiciously, smirking slightly, watching my hands. I slid them into my pockets. I slid them out again and then pushed my thumbs back in. Who did I think I was? Who did you think I was? I was the guy who looked out for you at parties. I minded the bottle so Seagull and A.J. wouldn't help themselves, just for five minutes while you nicked out to the shed for a quick bong. Sometimes it was longer than five minutes, if you pashed someone. There's nothing in it, you said, because I was standing beside you when you got it on with Angus. It's just nice to have someone's tongue in your mouth for the rush.

You finished your smoke and flicked it under the brown tree ferns. I watched the glowing butt for a second or two and I asked myself what I was doing. I was being there: Mr Rock Steady. I'd always been here, only you'd never looked at me before, not dead on, not deadpan, because I'd made myself straight and narrow, like a goalpost. I'd been afraid of everything. I'd planted myself on the cusp of the long-gone.

What is the long-gone anyway? It's just two words, stuck together, with a meaning all its own, and I wondered if that's what would happen in the future. I wondered if all the words would come together and mean new stuff, until there was only one thing to know, one all-knowing thing. Maybe the one thing wouldn't mean anything at all, and that would be the end of the world, the end of everything, because nothing would make sense, nothing would mean anything.

I was being a freak, I knew it. I was pretending I wasn't left of centre—it was no use. That's where I went wrong.

See you Monday, you said.

I stood there, on the edge of everything, on the verge of the long-gone. I didn't say anything. I looked straight at you. I wasn't embarrassed by the stillness. I could do stillness. I could do anything if it would keep you from slipping through my fingers.

It's only early, I said. Do you want to watch TV for a bit or do you want to go to bed?

It was a slip of the tongue. You sucked the air in like you were going to laugh and then you coughed it out. I was going red. It was dark; you couldn't see. I'd have loved to ask you to go to bed with me, of course I would have, although I didn't think that was something you'd ask, not in words. I thought those words would be long gone and it would just happen.

I don't really have people over, you said, because of my mum. She's …

I don't care, I said. I won't tell anyone.

You lit another cigarette. Hmm, you said, puffing steadily, considering.

My parents are as strange as they come, I said, and they're roaming around like it's everyone's business.

You laughed. You still looked reluctant to let me in, so I had another crack at reassuring you. My parents are freaks, I said. My life is skew, too.

Skew? What sort of a word is that? You smiled and it was an easy smile and your eyes were in it, too. Usually, your eyes were dead when you smiled.

Wait there, you said, flicking the butt of your cigarette into the garden and heading inside. You closed the door behind you. When you came back, you said: You can come in for a bit. But if my mum comes out of her room, you have to leave, just get up and go. Don't say a word. Nothing.

We sat on the couch and you skimmed through the channels on the remote. I put my hand on your leg. You shifted, resting your head on my thighs and you wrapped your arms around my knees. I began to stroke your hair and you fell asleep. I was scared to move.

After an hour or so your mum came out. I'd never seen her before. She was wearing baggy underpants and a loose-fitting singlet. She looked like a hooker. *Sorry.* How would I know?

She looked like someone who has had a hard life and no money to take care of herself, like a broken woman at the end of the world, dead on her feet, skin slapped over her bones like white paint, old white paint, slightly yellow. Her shoulders and collarbones were sticking out of her skin like ... like nothing. There is nothing I know that is as awful as her bones poking out of her dirty yellow chicken-skin.

Sorry, this sounds shithouse ... I'm trying to explain.

She stared at me like I was a mirage, here and long gone, and I held up my hand and mouthed the word: Hi. I swallowed noisily and I told myself that I didn't care how she looked because I didn't want to care.

She stared at me for a good while and then she held her hand up and waved. The hair under her arm was black. The hair on her head was orange-blonde, wiry, like broken guitar strings. The darker, underarm hair ran down the midline of her scalp. She turned away from me, leaving the room as murkily as she had come. I thought of what people said about the smarmy sea and I didn't want to be like them.

When you woke up, you said: I love Mum. I'm not ashamed of her. Don't think I am. I don't want you to see her because you'll think that I can't love her because she's so fucked up. She looks disgusting; really she's beautiful.

You sat up. You were crying. You said: People look different when you love them.

I saw your mum, I said quickly. She came out before.

You gasped, white, panic-stricken. You put your head in your hands.

I couldn't move because you were asleep, I said, floundering. I worried that I was losing you and I never really had you—if you want something that much it feels like you have it. Almost.

You put your head down again, crying, wet-breathing. You held your head in your slimy hands and gagged on your tears. It sounded like gargling, like you were swallowing air and water in the grimy, wrong-town sea.

I can see the love, I said. I desperately wanted to believe what I was saying and it was true when I looked at you. Problem was: I couldn't reconcile it with the wreckage of your mum: burnt out, long gone, doped up and elsewhere.

I'm going to wash and trim her hair, you said, and dye it back to her natural colour: warm blonde with shiny gold streaks. I'll get the orange wrongness out of it. It makes her skin look yellow. It's not yellow, only her hair makes it look that way because it's a cheap colour. She should have let me do it. I would have done a better job, and massaged her scalp with some nice conditioner.

You were talking fast, swatting the tears away like flies. I kissed you because I had no words. It was our first kiss. It was long, like a long, salty conversation, like you understood perfectly what I was trying not to say.

She's really beautiful, you said. If she had another life she would have been in magazines. It's the greyness that makes her look awful. If you take the sickness away, I mean the shadows and her hard life …

She would look like you, I said. I couldn't see it, not really, but I could believe it. Believing without seeing is long and gone.

Mum said: It will end in tears; it will never work and I believed her because I was scared. I was soft as. Mum said your family were different, not like us: fringe people. She spoke as if you were from the dark side, another life form, and I wondered what Jesus and the lepers would make of that. I believed Mum because I let myself believe her and that has come back to haunt me because you and I had something crucial and Mum is a mystery to me.

When I thought about my future with you it was like seaweed around my neck: thick, flat and rubbery. They say that's why the beach smells on the wrong side of town, because they have all the seaweed.

At the start, I thought I would love you forever, even if you ended up like your mum. I thought: How could I stop? I thought I could protect you and we wouldn't go under. I thought I could stop you rotting in your own living body. In the end, I couldn't get past the fear that you would wind up all ratty: broken and hollow … fucked like your mum.

I was weak. I was scared of what you would become. I was afraid of the unknown, and there's nothing more long gone than being frightened of something that might never happen. I shook you off like a cold wind, steeling myself and telling myself that the crying was just a stage. I'm not strange or left of centre anymore. I didn't even tell you why. I didn't know. I ran hard into the long-gone, pretending I'd done my best by you.

As time went by, you hardly came to school. Sometimes I walked home via your place, just in case. I never saw you. I wondered if I had imagined you, conjured you. I lurked in front of your house for a while and I thought I could smell your shampoo, lilting in the wind. It was probably just the smell of clean, wet washing, blowing in the breeze on the wrong side of town.

I couldn't smell the stench that everyone talked about. Everyone said the wrongness was there. I didn't have the nose for it, I guess.

If I start this letter again now it will be different. And so it goes. I have decided to send it. Maybe you remember these things the same way. Perhaps you will never forgive me.

I'm sorry, Chelsea. I'm so sorry and it's not enough.

Geoff.

Chapter Five

The riddling

Riddle: —noun

1. a question or statement so framed as to exercise one's
ingenuity in answering it or discovering its meaning;
conundrum

Dictionary.com

The package is addressed to Mum, but I've been in charge of
the mail and the bills forever so I open it without a thought.

Inside the package is a melamine plate with a child's drawing on it. There are five people in the picture. Their names
are written there: Mum—Chelsea—Teddy—Pelts—Dean.

There is a note. It says:

Dear Annie,

*You gave me this plate all those years ago and I have kept it,
hanging in my kitchen.*

*I still want to be in the picture. It's all I think about. It's all I've
thought about, these many years.*

Pelts

I decide I'll go to the market. I'll take the plate to the fortune
gypsy. Then I'll show it to Mum …

The gypsy says: Give me your hand. Her voice is seductive, hypnotic. I could listen to her whisper her strange little secrets forever. She has all the answers and I'm desperate because I have no idea how to help Mum. She can see it all, the past and the future. She can see everything. I'm falling for her. I've fallen. I'm obsessed. She's the only one who can help me.

The sign draped over the front of the tent says: Amadika's Tent of Fortune. Even the name makes me quiver. There are blankets and shawls everywhere, draped across her body, hanging from the walls of the tent, scattered across the cushions and low folding chairs.

I ask her: Where did you get the blankets?

Aah, where did I get the blankets, a simple question you ask. Perhaps you really wish to know about the hands, the dreams that wove the blankets into being? What are they like, the people who craft these treasures with their nimble, human fingers? The blankets look like the work of more than human hands—no?

This is my wake-up call, my cue to respond. I'm not sure I understand so I don't say anything. The gypsy holds the shawls in her hands tenderly, as if they are alive. Although she speaks slowly, her voice isn't easy to understand. The words are woven together so that her English sounds like a secret language, a chant, a calling of spirits. Listening to her is like listening to my conscience, only jangled.

I crave the words she speaks and the way she speaks them. I try to remember what she says so that I can repeat it back to myself, but her words fall through my fingers. I can never remember them just so.

She is an oracle, a messenger. She knows how to save Mum.

To dress oneself is nothing but colours, she says, rearranging the shawls around her neck and staring at me with the black-glass eyes. To bear children is wealth, she adds. You ask your mammy. You ask Annie.

For a second I think I misheard because they sound the same: mammy and Annie. I can't speak so I stare at her, frightened and desperate.

Go, she says and I wonder where ten minutes went. I never know what happens to the time because it passes in slow and fast motion together, like a dream.

When I come out of the tent, Geoff takes my hands and rubs them between his own. He is trying to bring me back to him, trying to rub her off. I don't tell him anything. I wait for him to ask. I make him beg me for it.

What did she say?

She said there is a man in my life and he only wants sex.

Don't be ridiculous, he says, flashing me his dimple. Did she really mention me?

She says you are ripe inside like a watermelon, I tell him.

Did she say my name?

She doesn't usually say people's names, she …

Convenient, he says.

It's like a story, I say quickly, but I decide who is who.

She says the same thing to everyone, he says.

She does not! I say. You have bad breath, I add, turning away from him and walking towards the doughnut van. I turn back after a few steps: How could the same thing possibly be true for everyone? I say.

He is cupping his hands in front of his mouth and breathing into them, trying to smell his breath. He says: She manipulates words. She says the same lines over and over …

Shut up, I say.

Geoff thinks that it's unnatural to find out about the future, before time. He worries that I will adjust my behaviour, drawing myself towards that future as if nothing else is possible. Geoff thinks that the gypsy is meddling—fiddling with possibility as if it were a fixed thing, changing what might have been into something else altogether.

But it's all I have.

I'm possessed by the gypsy's words. I'm desperate because I think Mum's going to die. And what's so dangerous about believing in stories? What's the harm in believing things could be better?

A month passes before the market is on again. It's been a big month. Everything has changed so quickly, from grey to something else, shiny mother-of-pearl, the other side of grey, like an abalone shell. This last month, I've let myself believe things might be better and I don't want stories. Stories aren't enough anymore. I need straight answers.

These hands have been toiling for love, the gypsy says. Toiling; toiling; toiling for love. She holds my hands and I'm helpless. She can see the grey and I can't speak.

She makes toiling sound like a different word each time. My hands are resting in hers. She is standing and I am sitting so my hands are high above my head, as if I'm praying, paying homage to her. She lowers my hands as she speaks and they feel heavier with each lowering, as if she is levering them down, as if she knows things about me that she shouldn't know.

Don't throw away the milk pails, she says. A tear rolls down my cheek and she reaches over and wipes it with her cold, soft thumb, too cold to be part of a living body, too soft to be a human hand. It means your hope, she says, your last hope.

She pulls a small wooden box across the table—it is filled with small bottles. She turns my hands over so that my palms are facing up. She takes one of the bottles and pours two perfect drops onto each of my wrists and then she rubs them briefly in a circular motion. The oil smells like sandalwood.

She takes another bottle—one drop for each of my wrists this time—I think it is lemon. Lemon myrtle, she says, as if she's reading my mind. I close my eyes. I can smell freshly cut wood and wildflowers and I open my eyes to make sure I am where I think I am.

The gypsy pours clear oil into her hand from a large bottle and then she sets the bottle aside. She rubs her hands together, lathering them in the oil. Her hands are wrinkly and smooth. The wrinkles are fine, grey-white, like spider webs across her coffee skin.

Close your eyes, she says, one word spilling into the other as she takes my hand, pushing her fingers into my flesh. She begins at the wrist, pressing against the oil, muttering in a whisper. Her voice multiplies. She works her way into the palm of my hand, down each of my fingers. She is singing a soft song, continuous foreign words: too many sounds for one voice, like she's singing with her sisters.

The maker of a song does not spoil it, she says. She pauses, breathing with a rattle as if she might cough. You understand, no?

I nod, murmuring: Yes. I am crying. She turns me inside out. I want to know what she sees.

No one should interfere because you understand your own business.

Yes, I say, keeping my eyes closed, crying steadily.

The gypsy pushes hard against my palm, near the base of my thumb. The pain stabs as her fingers dig deep, biting my flesh, like pincers. I think the pain is good, for my own twisted good.

I open my eyes briefly because I can't bear the pain. I want to check if she has a knife, something sharp; it's only the ball of her knuckled thumb. She waits for me to close my eyes and then she starts talking again.

She says: You don't take shelter from the rain in a pond. You are smart—no?

Yes, I say.

Don't worry if your work is behind closed doors: Watch me was carried off by a crocodile.

I will be careful, I say.

No! she says, yelling, sounding like an everyday angry person. Do *not* be careful; only be true to yourself. The dying of the heart is a thing unshared. These things are always behind doors.

She presses on my other hand now. Her thumbs push hard against my palm. The pressure shoots straight from my hand to my temple. I feel it surge up through my arm, my shoulder, my neck. I wonder whether the gypsy is using her hands to imprint herself on my mind.

I listen to see if she will continue. I want her to stop and I never want it to end. The ache in my temple becomes sharp, fierce. I can't bear it. I open one eye. She is watching me, waiting for me. I am in love with her—I'm obsessed, possessed—it's all torment and desire.

You understand—no?

Yes, I say, quickly, desperately. I close my eyes tight. I scrunch them together until I see shards of light, shattered, splintered mother-of-pearl …

Go, she says, placing my hands on the table.

I panic. Is she sending me away? That can't have been ten minutes. I feel gutted, scared as shit, and I fire my question at her. My mum, I say. Is she going to die?

The gypsy gasps. I have surprised her as I have surprised myself. I have practised this question, last night, again this morning. I had every intention of asking it, only I didn't know if I would go through with it.

I speak louder, angrily: *Is Annie going to die?* It's the voice I use for Grandad, the voice that means: Don't you even think about fucking with me.

I fossick around in my bag and bring out the picture-plate with the big yellow sun and the blue sky and the bluer water and the smiling stick figures. I touch the figures; I trace the figure of Mum, then myself, and finally the phantom figures: Teddy and Dean and Pelts.

Someone called Pelts sent this to my mum, I say. He says he still wants to be in the picture. Obviously, he knows who these people are. He knows who they are to me. The picture-plate is all smiles: a happy-family picture of strangers. I give the plate to the gypsy, crying hard, and I say: Who are these people? … *Please!* Is Annie going to die?

The gypsy says: There is no time to waste … for the earth does not get fat.

What does that mean? I say. What do you mean?

I cannot tell you what I mean, she says. Only what I know … There is a death on the water, she says. A death. Deathly. Death. And the earth does not get fat.

Today there's nothing I can tell Geoff. There's nothing to say.

Another month passes and the market is on again. I am even more determined to get some proper answers. I want the gypsy to tell me about the death on the water. I want specific details. Names.

We stand at the gate and Geoff hunts in his pockets for some coins to pay the entry fee. Grandad holds onto his arm. I'm all set to run ahead as soon as we get through the gate.

All the regular stalls are there, just the same as last time, unaltered, like a picture, like déjà vu, except I can't see the gypsy's tent. I feel sick, concrete in my stomach, the suffocating heaviness I've known a couple of times when I couldn't wake Mum, when I couldn't register the sound or movement of her breathing, vivid for a split second and then gone, so gone.

I scan the stalls again, but the gypsy's tent is nowhere in sight. I think maybe she's moved to a quieter spot because usually she's right beside the food vans and it gets very noisy. I scan the walkways for the peak of black canvas. I walk quicker, then run.

I look back at Geoff and wish I hadn't. He glances at me, distracted. Grandad is handling fragile items, hand-blown glass, dazzling colours. Geoff tries to take the glass from Grandad, talking all the while.

I can't watch them. I don't want to help. I run away as fast as I can. I imagine I see the gypsy's black hood near the toilet block and I hurry in that direction. I'm breathless, swallowing mother-of-pearl splinters and abalone dreams. Grey.

The tent isn't there. The gypsy isn't there. I pass the stalls quickly. Everything blurs together like the ti-tree out of the bus window.

There are a couple of little laneways with a few small stalls in each. The laneways lead to portable classrooms: music rooms, art rooms. Today these rooms are abuzz with children's face painting and fairy-floss machines, but the gypsy isn't there. I want to tell the kids that the fun is a farce: the colours and the sweetness are a big fucking lie. I have no time because I've got to keep searching for the gypsy.

Perhaps she's sick. Perhaps she's dead. I wonder whether she can foresee her own death or whether her visions are just for strangers. She must see her own future, too. How could the mind distinguish? Maybe the gypsy knew she was going to die and that's why she told me about the unfat earth and the death on the water, only I don't understand because the puzzle is missing some pieces. I need the gypsy to fit it together. All that I have is a happy-family picture-plate, a bunch of strangers in a memory I don't know.

I run now, covering the market in a handful of minutes. I know she's not there. I end up back where I started, back where the gypsy should be, where she always was. Geoff and Grandad are waiting and I don't want to be near them. I want to run away from everyone who needs me.

Grandad is grinding his feet into the bitumen, marching furiously on the spot. His face is wet with tears and foaming spit, ugly neediness.

He broke a window decoration, a butterfly leadlight, says Geoff. I had to pay for it.

I want some doughnuts, bawls Grandad.

I don't have any money left, says Geoff emptily.

When Grandad gets upset like this, he mourns everything that he has ever been sad about in his life. Usually he cries about Mum. He thinks that I am Mum and he loves me and he hates me, more than I can bear. I can't help him because it's all a story in his mind and I am pleasure and pain to him, and he begs me to bring the children home. He says it over and over and I say: Of course I will, I'm on my way, just to settle him.

When he's like that, I can't do anything to help him and people stare at us like they want to call the police or an ambulance. Most times I smile, and if they keep staring I explain that he has dementia, but today I'm caught up in the loss of the gypsy and I don't want to explain.

A woman with bright-red lipstick approaches us. She takes the red scarf from around her neck and she wipes Grandad's tears. Her shiny black curls bounce around in the wind. She says: Can I help? She's gleaming: health and happiness and shiny red.

You can't do anything, I say. I'm sobbing. She touches my arm and I flinch. Go away, I say, just piss off. There's no anger in it because I'm too exhausted. Geoff tries to calm Grandad down. He's too far gone.

I'm a nurse, honey, says the woman with the red scarf. I work with people who have dementia. Confused people are my thing. She reaches for my hand again and smiles. What you are doing—it's hard work, really hard work. She takes hold of my hand and I weep, remembering that the gypsy is gone.

The lady with the red scarf takes a pen out of her handbag. She writes her name and phone number on the back of a card. If you need some help with him, she points to Grandad, you ring me, honey, okay?

She puts her hand on my shoulder, near my neck, as if she's known me her whole life, as if I'm her child, but then she's gone and Grandad is still losing it, and today I don't want to pacify him, today I want him to shut the fuck up. I could kill him with my own bare hands, drown him (Is it Grandad? Is he the death on the water? Am I capable of it?).

I want to be free enough to thrash around, to sob and bellow and cry. I want Geoff to console me. I want someone like the shiny-red lady to look after Grandad, just for one day, so I can look after myself, so I can have a few gin and tonics and do whatever I want.

I give Geoff the money that I had for the gypsy and he takes Grandad to buy some doughnuts. When we are back on the bus, Grandad becomes quiet. The vibration of the bus engine seems to soothe him and he stares out of the window in silence.

He looks over at me, briefly, and I can see that he is back in the now. He has one doughnut left in the bag and sugar sparkles around his mouth. He sucks the air in sharply because he's still rattled from the crying, but he's smiling all the same. He holds up his doughnut bag to show me, grinning from ear to ear. His eyes are shiny from the crying, gleaming from the joy of hot doughnuts, razzled and wonderful and sad and stupid.

I sit beside Geoff, swinging my legs around and resting them on his thighs, my back against the window. She wasn't there, I say. I ran around the whole market.

I know, says Geoff. I went to the lost-and-found tent where they take the bookings. That's it for her, they reckon. She didn't re-book.

I lurch, thinking I'll vomit, but I just get a mouthful of bile. All I can do is go home, and when I get there, everything looks stupid and useless. The house smells of simmering bolognese and hopeless love.

It's four o'clock, close enough to the end of the day for a drink, and far enough away from happiness to have a crack at happy hour. I mix myself a gin and tonic; I mix two, kidding myself that I'm making one for Geoff. He shakes his head when I hold it out to him. Mr Pure. Grandad looks exhausted. He doesn't understand money. If you don't buy him a doughnut, he thinks you're being mean.

I feel like the gypsy died, and unless she is dead, in the irreversible physical sense, then I'm pissed off that she didn't come. She knows I need her. I want to unwind and forget her, but how can I forget that there is a death on the water (that there was, or there will be)? I need to know what it means (the dying of the heart, the unfat earth). I think it means that Mum is doomed. I need to know more. I need to know how to save her.

I go to the bedroom to tuck Grandad in only to find he's already asleep. I feel like the biggest bitch in the world—a ride on the bus, a warm jam doughnut, that's his perfect day, it's child's play, but it got ugly and I didn't tell him it was okay, and I didn't tell him a story about next time or tomorrow, a story that would make him forget our shitty life.

Today I watched him lose it, crying and gabbling, and I didn't try to pull him out of it. I didn't tell him about the lovely dinner I had ready for him, about the chocolate ice cream I had in the freezer for his dessert.

I kiss him on his pale, sun-spotted forehead. I smooth my tears along his wrinkles with trembling fingers.

When I come out of Grandad's room, Geoff is waiting near the front door. He has his coat on. I should go, he says.

Oh, I say.

I put my hands around his waist, under his shirt, and I kiss him. It's a needy kiss. Come and lie down for a bit, I say. When we are stretched out on my bed, I tell Geoff about the unfat earth. I say I am worried about a death and I mention the water. I don't tell him I'm quoting the gypsy. I own the words as if they were mine and perhaps he thinks they are although, of course, they could only be hers.

We stretch out on my bed, gazing up at the stars that are scattered across my ceiling. We could be anywhere. The stars are stickers, they glow in the dark and they look surprisingly real, especially after a couple of gutsy gin and tonics. I put my hands on Geoff's chest. I love chests. Take off your shirt, I say. I want skin on skin, there's nothing like the comfort of it.

With Geoff, it's not just about the sex. I think he loves me and that's why I hold off on the sex. I think love and sex together will be complicated, but today I'm craving the comfort of the sex and so I pretend love isn't messy and broken.

Geoff falls asleep afterwards and I get up for a bit. I want to have a quick smoke, an after-sex smoke like in the movies. I suck the smoke down hard and wallow in the smack-bang physicality of the moment. I blow smoke up at the stars and pretend that I have a different life. I go inside and mix another drink. I wash the last of the dishes and wipe down the benches, top up my drink.

I better go, Sea, says Geoff. He is standing in the kitchen doorway, pulling his shirt over his head. I love that he calls me Sea, not Chelsea, not Shells. Sea means I can be anything.

Don't go, I say, sounding needy, and that's why I didn't want the love with the sex, that's why I don't want people helping me, in case it makes me needy.

I should go, I …

I move towards him, wrapping my arms around his back. He has very defined back muscles and they twitch beneath my fingers.

I just got up for a smoke, I lisp—that's the gin talking. I couldn't sleep, I say, speaking slowly and carefully. I didn't want to disturb you.

I should go, says Geoff again.

Please don't go, I say. Come back to bed.

Just for a minute, he says, kissing my forehead. We crawl back under the covers and have sex a second time. It's like another world, without the hurting love—so sad too because the shadow of his leaving lurks there like the broken grey shells.

Geoff sits on the edge of the bed and ties his shoes. Give me a second, I say. I'll come out for a smoke.

Don't worry, he says. Stay there. I'll lock the door when I leave.

I'm not desperate for a smoke, not really, I just want to hold onto him, to draw out the leaving. Anyway, I refuse to lie in bed and say goodbye when we've just had sex—that would be pathetic, like old, married people.

I get out of bed and pull on the dressing-gown that Mum gave me. It used to be hers. It's black and silky with pink rosebuds all over it. It's the most beautiful thing I have ever owned. It's a bit scrappy really, a few runs in the fabric that end in small fluffy balls, but it feels luxurious against my skin and it reminds me of the life Mum deserves, and it reminds me that Mum was someone else before she was so fucked up. I tie the dressing-gown across my waist and put on a pair of socks.

I light up as soon as we get out the front. As I blow the first drag up at the stars, a car pulls into the driveway. Odd, I say.

It's Mum, says Geoff, and Dad. I wonder how they knew I was here ...

What? I say (where else would you be?).

Hey. I'll catch you tomorrow, says Geoff, or Monday.

Monday? I say. There's not a day in the past couple of months that he hasn't been here, not one day. He was here on Christmas-fucking-Day for Christ's sake. Tonight we had sex—for the first time—for the second time ...

Under the garish headlights, my dressing gown turns to scamp-glitz. Geoff turns to me: See ya, he says.

See ya! Where's the Sea in see ya?

Geoff? I say.

Yeah?

Never mind, I say, and I realise how sad those words really are, such a very sad way to say: Don't worry about it.

Don't worry about it means: no sweat, whatever brother, all's well that ends well. Never mind means something else. Never mind means: Why didn't your parents know you were here? It means: Why didn't you kiss me goodbye? Never mind means: I mind, make no mistake, but perhaps you don't mind, perhaps you never minded—mind you, you were on the game, you had all the moves, like minding was all you were mindful of.

Geoff stops coming after that.

I decide to take some of Mum's pills and get sleepy in the bath Then I worry that I might be the death on the water, and what would happen to Mum and Grandad if I wasn't around to take care of them? So I stumble out of the bath and get dressed before I take the tablets.

I dose myself with a couple of the pills and a few more of the usuals. I line up the drinks on my bedside table, and skull them quickly, consecutively, savouring nothing, the nothing of the nothing.

I lie down on my bed and shake my legs irritably until the relaxers kick in. I open one of my eyes a moment later. It must be more than a moment because it's dark now. The moments have become long and short together and the gypsy is standing there, hovering beside my bed. It's windy and her clothes fly around her like blackbirds. The coloured scarves have gone. I try to tell her about Geoff. She can't understand me and I am angry that I have no control of my words: they are twisted and crumbling and they don't make sense.

You deserted me, I say to the gypsy. Fuck you, I add, reaching my hand out to her, but the blackbirds flutter and fall apart like ash.

What is the death on the water? I try to scream. I sound washed out and ashen like never mind.

Then the gypsy is gone, swallowed by the unfat earth and Geoff is there. I tell him all the things that I didn't tell him when my voice was working and he says: Never mind.

I lay still then, but I keep talking even though my words sound like they're underwater. I think that perhaps I have altered the future and changed the present, all because I wanted something that was never going to happen, a fairy-tale ending, where ugly things turn to mother-of-pearl.

And then there is no one. I wonder if they were here at all. I want to check on Mum ... I can't because my legs won't work.

What have you done to yourself? I yell. There is no one to never mind.

I put my fingers down my throat, pushing and prodding until I vomit. I reach over, grabbing the hairbrush from the bedside table and I shove the handle down my throat. I push it hard against the base of my tongue until I lurch and gag, straight over the edge of my bed, in my bed.

I try to get up. My legs fall apart under me. I crawl towards the door and down the hallway.

I bump the walls. I bash my head against the skirting board. I am frightened. If I don't sharpen up—if I fall asleep like this, I mightn't wake up at all.

I lunge forward again, arms first, *breathe-breathe-breathe*, and then I drag my demented legs and lunge forward again. I crawl into the bathroom and I pull myself up onto the edge of the bath. I pull myself up higher, lift a leg and fail, lift again, fail. Then I heave myself up, crying, and I land a leg over the edge of the bath and thump myself in.

The cold porcelain is something, a reward of sorts, *breathe-breathe-breathe*. I reach up and turn on the cold tap, just a dribble, and I lift my head and turn my neck, trying to catch some of the water in my mouth. I sip from the dribbling tap and vomit and vomit. I turn the tap up to get more pressure, only I am clumsy. There is too much water. I am freezing in my own vomit. I sob.

Is this the death on the water? Answer me, gypsy cunt, I yell, in my drowned voice. I vomit and I sip and I can barely swallow before I vomit again. It's in my hair, everywhere, and I think that I will probably die.

And Geoff can go and fuck himself and jerk off and take his bleeding fucken heart and offer it up to the Virgin Fucken Mary.

I don't care if I die, except for Grandad and Mum.

Probably it doesn't mean anything at all, the unfat earth, and probably the death on the water is a crock of ashen blackbird shit.

The next day I'm still alive and I know it can't go on. Something must change or we will all die. I decide to take charge like the unfat earth, because there's no one else to know or care or never mind.

I take the happy-family picture-plate of strangers and put it on the kitchen bench. I make sure the bench is clear and shiny-clean and I stand the plate there, between the salt and pepper, dead centre, on show, so Mum can't miss it.

Who are they? I say when she picks it up. She turns away from me. She takes the plate and walks towards her room.

I've just made it back from the dead. I've got dried vomit in my hair and I won't be ignored.

I charge at her and take the plate. She wrestles me for it, but she's a skinny nothing ghost and she can't wrestle. I hold it out to her and pull it away. I hold it out again, baiting her. She stands with her arms by her sides and her eyes bulge out of her yellow face, her cheekbones protruding and ridiculous. Her skin is like cheese, yellow and dead. Nothing about her is breathing. She is revolting and I hate her. I give her back the plate because she's pathetic and I say again: *Who are they?*

She looks at me with scared-shitless eyes. She drops the plate against the slate floor tiles and shuffles back to bed. She can't even lift her feet off the ground.

The plate shatters in one lightning break, slightly off centre, as I hurl it after her, hard, against the floor tiles. You pathetic, gutless fuck, I say. She doesn't even turn around.

I take the broken plate and put it back in the post pack that it arrived in. I re-read the letter from the phantom Pelts.

I write directly underneath his message:

I am in the picture and I know who I am.

You say you want to be in the picture (I underline 'in the picture'). *Who the fuck are you?*

Chelsea

I seal the envelope and write: RETURN TO SENDER.

I feel all smashed up. I believed in the gypsy and I believed in Geoff. With all my heart I believed in them and where did it get me? Wallowing in my own vomit. So fuck pictures, fuck everything.

Chapter Six

Beyond the point of no return

Point of no return:
The point in a course of action beyond
which reversal is not possible.

The American heritage dictionary of the English language, 4th edn,
Houghton Mifflin, http://www.yourdictionary.com/point-of-no-return

Pelts says: Bring her home, Shells. She needs to come back here.

I consider this, wondering if there's any way I can manage it.

I should never have let Annie leave, right after your brother died, he says, lighting a smoke and offering me one. I've just had a smoke, but I take it anyway because I want to breathe in the word 'brother'.

It didn't feel real, he says. It was easier to think that she'd taken Teddy with her when she left. It was impossible to believe that he was dead.

The cigarette smoke pours out of his mouth and nose as he speaks. He doesn't pause to blow it out. It was so fast, he says. First you were all here, then Teddy was dead and you were gone. Annie up and left on the heel of it all, so in my mind's eye I skipped the horrible end. I imagined you were all still together.

I'm smoking fast, giving myself a head spin. Pelts's ciggies are a lot stronger than mine and I feel tingly and sweaty, like I might throw.

I was still there, you see, so I had all the happy memories. Annie disappeared fast and it was like she took the horror with her. Probably sounds stupid, but it's true. Dead set.

After she left, I would wander along the foreshore where all the beach boxes are. That's where we used to walk, and it reminded me of the good stuff. I'm no fucken psychologist, only she left straight after—she had no time to remember that there was good.

I feel like time has stopped. I'm aware of my breathing and the pulse in my neck. Everything else is still. I can't remember Teddy, not in pictures, and yet somehow he's a part of everything I know. I can feel him. I'm frightened to ask anything about him because, if I ask questions, he might vanish. If I push he might disappear.

I've always felt Teddy, you see. I just never understood that this walking-beside-myself feeling was my own brother. Now there are words for the shadowy sensation. It was real before yet untouchable, a smoky haunting that I couldn't shake. I understand what the ghosting is now only it's not enough. I want more—I'm scared shitless.

Pelts sucks hard on his cigarette, squashing the butt between his thumb and middle finger, squeezing a bit more out of it. Fuck me, the dreams we had, he says, his fingertips trembling. He ashes his ciggie with a firm *tap, tap* to shake off the quivering and a rattly laugh echoes out of him. He's scared too—we're both freaking out.

We'd walk past all the yuppy punks on their beach-box verandahs, sipping their gin and tonics and watching the sun disappear for the day. I'd tell Annie she deserved it all. I said it'd all be hers one day because she was so beautiful, absolutely fucken stunning and so good, so clear in her heart and tender to you kids, so fucken tender.

Pelts takes another intense suck on his fag, pauses again. She probably didn't know that I was dreaming it for me, too. It was impossible not to dream about being with her. She deserved everything and I wanted to give it to her because she was a pearler. Breaks my heart to hear she's so broken.

He pushes the butt into the ashtray, holding his breath and pressing firmly. Bring her home, Shells, he says, blowing the idea out fast with the smoke.

First things first, I think, as I rattle home on the bus. It's a great place to think really, nothing in the way of the thinking other than the stop-start of other passengers getting on and off.

I open my wallet and take out the card that Joan gave me last month. I remember her face. I have imagined her so many times that I have turned her into a shiny-red dream.

Probably she won't remember me. Probably it's too late to ask for help; still, I will ask and it will not be a dream. I will ask for Mum's sake, not for my own, because her life is a sack of horseshit, not even a life. If there is some good in returning her to the place where my brother died, I will do it, and of course I want to go there, too, so I can get a picture for this feeling that is Teddy.

I don't know how to say any of this to Mum because she never told me about Teddy, she never mentioned him, and yet he has always been moored between us. I'm frightened to talk about Teddy in case Mum gets worse, although I can't imagine how she could get any worse. I don't even know what worse would look like.

Pelts is right, we need to go back, and we need to do it before Mum is in the rip where I can't reach her. We need to do it before she's lost forever. Pelts told me about the rip, the treacherous passage of ocean between the heads. He knows about all the ships that were lost there and, if we're not talking about Mum, that's what we talk about, sea stories, because other people's history is safe ground.

Pelts spouts the stories like a sea prophet. He has loads of books; he even has paintings of some of the lost vessels. Just think, all those dead bodies swirling in the water, loved ones, all mixed up in the black wash, and no one knows how it ended for them.

I want to know where Teddy is buried. I want to know if I saw him die. Surely I would remember that, seeing your brother die must be unforgettable. Unanswered questions swirl in my stomach like bodies in the water and I know that there is a time limit. I know that if the tide changes I may not be able to get Mum back. Teddy will be lost to me forever and Mum will be too deep, too far out, beyond the point of no return.

If I lose Mum then I'll have no one. Well, there is Pelts, but he's more like the gatekeeper because the actual memories belong to Mum and perhaps to me, except that I can't remember them. At last everything feels like it's beginning to fit together in the right way and yet at the same time it's more wrong than ever.

I force myself to call Joan because there's nothing left, nothing other than the sure feeling that Mum will die. I pick up the phone in a panic, wondering whether I'm already too late.

When I hear Joan's voice I lose it completely, spilling my guts and blathering into the phone. I can barely get the words out and I have them written on a piece of paper. I am so relieved that she is actually real and I didn't imagine her. I am frightened that she won't be able to help me.

I saw you at the market last month, I tell her. You were wearing a red scarf. I pause because clearly the scarf is irrelevant. I laugh at myself, just one laugh and then I stop because I'm laughing and crying together and she'll think craziness runs in the family.

My grandad was crying. He was hysterical, I say. You gave me your number …

I need help with him so that I can take Mum away, just for a week, two at the most. If I don't take her now I will lose her forever and then I'll have no one.

Joan barely has time to say: I remember you. I'm not used to asking for help and I'm out of my skin. I'm frightened that people will find out that I'm responsible for Mum and Grandad. I'm frightened they'll think I'm not capable and they'll take Grandad away for good. They'll send me back to school and lock Mum away somewhere. I feel this is the lesser of two evils. It's a trade-off—but still a desertion, a disloyal, hideous walking away.

Can someone mind Grandad? I sob. Someone nice. Somewhere safe, where he can't wander off. He's mostly really easy as long as you explain what's going to happen before it happens, otherwise he panics. He loves bolognese, spaghetti bolognese. It's his favourite.

Joan says: Chelsea, it's okay. It's going to be okay. I'm going to come and see you later today. I finish work at five. Give me your address. Don't go cleaning up or anything. Not for me. I'll be there after work and we'll sort it out. When do you need to go? It's going to be okay, honey. *Trust me.*

As it turns out, respite care is an option for Grandad. I don't have to book him in to a nursing home permanently. I am entitled to four weeks of respite relief per calendar year, as long as Grandad is assessed as meeting the criteria, and that's Joan's job so she says don't worry about that. She does the paperwork on the spot; she says that's the easy part.

She brings hot coffee for us, a warm chocolate for Grandad, and a cardboard tray of little cakes, custard tarts with glazed strawberries, chocolate éclairs, vanilla slice. Grandad eats them while we talk and I fall in love with Joan.

I realise that there are angels. They are real people, walking and breathing among us. Forget about religion and bearded prophets, I'm talking about a real woman in jeans and a silky floral shirt, someone who lives her work and works her life with the same enormous heart, loving strangers like they are her own people, flesh-and-blood love, patting Grandad's hand and cleaning the cake off his chin, making him laugh like they're old pals—that's Joan, my angel, and I will love her until the day I die.

I tell Grandad that it's Joan's job to make holidays for people and that he has been picked to have a turn. I tell him that there will be people to play cards with him, just like Geoff used to do, but more people, all his own age, and music concerts and lovely food, lots of lovely food, and ladies to make cups of tea for him, a real holiday.

Grandad says: Are you coming with me?

Five fucking words. Break my fucking heart.

No, I say. It's for people like you, people who have worked hard their whole life and earned a holiday.

I will go if you say, he says.

Six words, gutting me senseless, so that for a moment I think the dementia isn't real. I imagine that he can switch it on and off because, in that hideous moment, he understands everything. He understands that I am abandoning him and that I have no choice, and he says okay because he knows that I would never do this if there was another way. For those few moments, it's like he's back from the land of the confused; he is perceptive and rational and kind; he's really back, just for a minute. I'm overcome and I try to explain it to him.

I need to get Mum better, I say. She'll die if I don't help her.

The moment is gone. Grandad stands at the window, one hand against the glass. The wind in the magnolia tree flutters like purple-and-white birds and Grandad fiddles distractedly with his balls. Perhaps he sees past the strange birds to another time. Perhaps in his mind's glazed eye he sees a time and place he knows like the fluttering, somewhere purple and white, only he just has no words for purple-and-white places; there is no language for it.

I ring Pelts and I tell him we'll come. You'll need to pick us up, I say. I have to sort Grandad out first and then we'll come. She's bad, I say. I have told him that Mum was sad although I didn't explain how grave things really are. She's really bad, I sob. The person that you tell me about—that's not her anymore. The really beautiful one that you talk about, she's gone. You can't judge her. Don't be disappointed by her because she can't help it—she's gone past the point.

Somehow, it's easier to tell Pelts the whole ugly truth over the phone. Then I don't have to see him suffer for it as well. I don't know if anyone can help her, I say. She can't get up for days at a time and her hair is greasy and her breath is bad. She can't talk to you and her eyes can't look at you, and her skin is yellow and wrong. Promise me you won't think she's disgusting and horrible. She's my mum. You can't be mean to her because she can't help that she looks revolting.

I love her, Shells, he says and he's crying too. I could never be mean to her. I've loved her forever.

She might fight us, I say. I've never tried to take her anywhere. I've never made her get out of bed or leave the house. She might fight.

We'll cross that bridge if and when, he says. I hear the metallic churn of the flint as he lights a smoke. He doesn't wrap his lips around the butt properly and I hear a whistling sound as he sucks it in.

I've waited years for her to need me, he says, blowing smoke into the phone, like a gust of wind. I've never been game to move or even go on a holiday in case she showed up. You say the word, he says. I'm there.

Taking Grandad to respite care is horrible. It's a week to the day since I first talked to Joan and people usually wait months. Joan said there was an unexpected opening and I was on the emergency list. She pulled some strings of course. Grandad cries when I say that I'm leaving. The crying turns to bellowing and he thrashes around, whacking Joan in the face, knocking her glasses hard into her nose. Joan takes off her glasses and it looks as though someone has clamped the bridge of her nose, puncturing it on either side. Blood drips down to her mouth. It's okay, Ted, she says. Her eyes are watering, washing down her face so that it looks like she's crying blood. Chelsea will be back soon, honey. It's morning-tea time now and we have chocolate cake today. I'm going to make sure you get a really big piece.

Joan turns to me. You go whenever you're ready, she says quietly, wiping blood from the corner of her mouth. I won't leave him alone. I'll stay with him.

He'll be really tired if he's had a blowout like this, I say. He'll need a sleep in the afternoon. He gets weepy after he lashes out because he's sorry although he can't remember why.

Joan takes my hand. I will love him for you, Chelsea, she says. I promise.

I kiss Grandad on the head. He is still and he doesn't respond. I love you, I say, patting his hand; I'm talking to Joan, too. I kiss Grandad, once on each cheek and then on his head. He likes to look out the window at the trees, I say.

Then that's what we'll do, says Joan. We'll have tea and cake near the garden window. You can have my cake, too, Teddy. Don't tell anyone. It's our secret.

I heard that, says one of the other residents. He is all smarted up in charcoal slacks and a green shirt and tie, different shades of green. His thick, silver hair is slicked back, parted on the right. He is like something from another time.

Can't get anything past you, Bert, says Joan. Bert was a teacher for fifty years, at a boys' secondary school. Can't pull the wool over your eyes, can we, Bertie?

Best you get some ice on that nose as soon as possible, says Bert, wandering off to find a seat.

I'm glad Grandad is in a trance because if he could see Joan's bloody face he would take fright all over again. I squeeze his hand a last time and run. Between the respite care and the train station I stop, vomiting explosively into a bush. Grief vomit—fierce as fuck.

When Pelts arrives at my place I am sitting on the front step with a fag and a vodka-lime soda, crying softly, exhausted. Replacing lost fluid, I say, laughing, holding up the glass. He laughs too. I tell him about Grandad. I tell him that leaving him is the hardest thing I have ever had to do, the worst day of my life.

You could bring him to my place, says Pelts. He can come too. He lights himself a smoke. I flick mine into the fish ferns and he offers me another. Wait till you see her, I say, leaning my head against the cold house bricks.

Have a rest while you're with me, he says. Let me help you, Shells. Just sit on the beach and have a fucken rest.

I shrug my shoulders.

I owe you that much, he says. I knew your dad was an unstable motherfucker and I should have done something about it. God knows I feel responsible.

Was he that bad? I can't remember him.

We're all that bad, says Pelts. All of us, conundrum and contradiction, good and bad, the difference with him is that he made shitty choices or no choices at all. He was a lazy, bong-smoking, waste of space. He didn't look after you guys. He had no fucken idea how lucky he was—sorry.

It's okay, I say. I don't remember him. It makes me sorry for Mum, that's all, because she deserves someone to be good to her. You can't judge her. *Please*. She looks whacked out and disgusting. You have to remember that she's really beautiful.

We go inside. I have the bags packed next to the door. Pelts carries them out to the car. When he comes back in I've mixed us a drink and I pass him one. We clink our glasses together and drink them fast because we need to get this over with.

Mum's eyes are open when we go in and I walk towards her. She's just a crease under the covers, a nothing, skinny and lifeless. Her hair is strewn around her bony face and her mouth is open and still. Against the white pillowcase, her teeth look grey, her face pancake yellow. Her wide, blank eyes stare at the veneer wardrobe.

We're going on a holiday, I say through nervous tears. Mum doesn't move, she doesn't look like she's breathing and I panic that she's already dead—I've left it too long. I rush over and push my hands down hard on her chest. She squirms slightly and I kiss her, my stomach knotting with relief—the horrible reality of her wretchedness.

I've brought someone to see you, I say, considering the misery afresh through Pelts's eyes. My voice is shaky and I'm crying wildly. We're going on a holiday.

Mum doesn't respond. Pelts moves up behind me. Hi, gorgeous, he says, kissing Mum on the head. I'm taking you girls to my place for a rest. I've been waiting for you to call me, Annie, so many years I've waited for you to ask me to come, and I can't wait anymore. He pushes Mum's awful greasy hair away from her face and kisses her head again. It's my turn to look after you now.

Pelts scoops Mum up in his arms, doona and all. She drops her head against his chest. I thought she would fight, but seeing her in Pelts's arms makes me realise that was impossible. The fighting is over and done. I only hope we're not past the point.

Every morning, Pelts goes into Mum's room and carries her to the bath, washing her hair and her body. She lolls in his arms like a dead doll. Pelts brushes her teeth and her fragile gums bleed as she spits into a glass. It's more like a dribble really; she can't even spit.

At the end of the first week he shaves her legs. I walk past the bathroom door and catch sight of him holding one of her legs out of the water, running a razor carefully along her calf. Is she smiling? Or is it only the morning light and the dimpled glass of the bathroom window, catching her face unevenly?

After the bath, Pelts takes Mum into the lounge and settles her on the long leather couch, putting cushions behind her head and a blanket over her legs. He gets most of the wet out of her hair with a blast from the blow dryer, and then he brushes it carefully and ties it in a ponytail. You used to wear it like this all the time, Annie-girl, he says, driving me crazy because you're so fucken beautiful.

I glance at him the first few times he says those things because I think he's doing it for me. I think he's talking to her like that because I didn't want him to think she was revolting, and yet he doesn't seem to worry whether I'm there or not.

He talks to her, patting and kissing her, puffing up her pillows. The lounge has big windows and he turns the couch on an angle to catch all the sun, kissing her again. Right, he says, clapping his hands once and rubbing them together. Breakfast.

I am showered, up and about, and I barely know what to do with myself without Grandad stalking me. Uninterrupted showers, that's my idea of a holiday, twenty minutes, longer if the water doesn't run out. I had imagined I'd be busy with Mum, but Pelts has taken her on and I feel as if there's no place for me. No one needs me and I'm not sure what to do.

I make a pot of tea and Pelts cooks bacon, eggs and sausages. I'm not much for big breakfasts so I just have a piece of toast. He cooks enough for the three of us and he manages to get some into Mum. He talks and talks until she opens her mouth and eats for him, and then he eats whatever's left, talking all the while, reading the paper and chatting about the news, about the bright-orange egg yolks, about what a great local butcher he has: Best sausages on the peninsula by a long shot.

He doesn't mind that Mum doesn't respond; he keeps it rolling along, calling her Annie-girl and sweetheart and telling her how beautiful she is all the time. He says: You going for a walk, Shells?

I nod, as if that had been my plan all along, and he passes this on to Mum, as if she can't hear because she doesn't speak. Hear that? Shells is off for a walk down the beach, just like you used to do, Annie-girl, traipsing around like a sheep dog. Don't tell me you don't remember that. You had all the energy in the world. I couldn't keep up.

That first day Pelts gives me some cash and asks me to buy a few things for dinner on the way back. Don't rush, he says, I don't need to get the lamb on until two or three. Buy yourself some lunch and something nice, a new top, a pair of shoes, a polka-dot bikini, whatever you want.

And that's the routine, locked in on day one, breakfast and morning sun together, then I disappear for four or five hours and later we have dinner together and watch the sun go down, early dinner and some red wine, maybe a fire if it's cold or just for the sake of it. Best holiday of my life.

I don't know what happens during the day because I'm not there, and when I arrive back, mid-afternoon, Pelts's greeting is always the same: Better get cracking with the dinner, then ay?

Sometimes I peel and chop the vegetables. We have a beer and chat about where I've been. Pelts yells it all out to Mum, waking her up if she starts dozing off. He tries to keep Mum awake during the day so that she can sleep at night without so many pills. It's a relentless commitment. He picks her up and carries her outside if she looks sleepy. He takes her out into the sandy sea air, talking to her all the while. He places her on the thick grass and picks up a ti-tree branch, or a flowery stem of the Chilean jasmine that grows along the fence. See how the leaves droop down and then curl back up at the bottom, just like the sea nettles I showed you in the book. Hold it, Annie. Smell it, he says, placing it in her hand.

Sometimes he is busy getting dinner ready and so he calls out to her, loudly, insistently, so she doesn't doze off. Did you hear that, Annie-girl? Shells has bought a new shirt, light blue. Then he nods at me: Put it on—go on—show your mum.

Some days Pelts won't let me help with the dinner. He says: Leave this to me. It's nice having people to cook for. Have a bath, put your feet up and read the paper, grab yourself a beer. I've got this.

After dinner, with full bellies and a glass of wine, we all sink a bit lower in our chairs. Pelts holds Mum's glass up to her lips and sometimes she takes a small taste. He launches the past, sets it sailing into the room like a pretty yacht and I can't keep my eyes off. I can't remember how he starts because there's no ruckus, nothing staged. Suddenly, the past is sailing in front of my eyes and I'm not sure where it came from.

Mostly he talks about Mum, about how hard she worked and about Teddy and me. At first, when he mentions Teddy, Mum cringes. She glances at me, wide-eyed, and then she cries for a while, curling herself into a ball and facing the back of the couch.

You have a good cry, Annie-girl. I don't think you ever had the chance for that. He was a fucking great kid.

I love that Pelts distinguishes between fucken and fucking. Fucken is an everyday descriptive, but fucking is special; he saves it for the big stuff.

Mum cries louder and Pelts keeps talking. He acted like a little man. And yet he was so young. It breaks me. His dad was as useless as tits on a bull. Teddy tried to make it right. He made up for that sack of shit ten times over. He was always helping you out with Shells, and you've got every reason to sob your guts out about that Annie-girl. You gave him every bit of love you had and I've never known anyone as full of love, 'cept Shells, he says, throwing me a wink. She's a gem alright.

Pelts moves the tapestry rocking chair a bit closer to Mum's long couch. He pats her forehead and strokes her hair and she cries more quietly. It's okay, my angel. It's my fault things are so hard. I should never have let you go away by yourself, just after you lost your boy and no one to look after you. That's my fault and I'll make it up to you for the rest of your life. I shouldn't have let you go.

Pelts refills our wineglasses. No one speaks, so he goes on. It's as bad as what Dean did—me letting you go. I didn't do anything to stop you leaving and that's as bad as all the shit he did, or didn't do. Lazy son of a fuck.

I start asking questions. I want to know everything, of course I do, and Pelts can only tell me that Teddy drowned. He says my father—Dean—took me away from the beach and Teddy drowned. He says that the rest is Mum's story. And you'll have to tell her soon, Annie, he says, while she can still see and touch all the places you're talking about, before climate change ups its ante and the Mornington Peninsula disappears altogether.

I say: Is it true, that it'll go under? I am panicking that I'll never know where my brother is buried.

Ten feet by 2050 they reckon, says Pelts, and Mum looks at us both intently, as if we're speaking a different language and her life is on the line. C'mon, Annie, you gotta tell Shells. They're her stories, too, after all, and the waves don't stop washing in for anyone.

Then he starts on something new, like Dean being a useless lazy fucker, or Bullser screwing the town with dope, and so it goes, night after night. During the day I walk and walk in lost time, picking up seashells and turning them over in my palm, sitting on the shore and rubbing my hands through the shell-gritty sand, hoping Teddy will wash in. I cry for Grandad, lost in his own time. Two weeks come and go like the tide as I am pulled between past and present.

I have to go back to Grandad, I say as we sit around together, empty plates at our feet. I am interrupting the onset of the past, but I have no choice because Grandad's absence is like the undertow, as strong as the pull of the past, and I need him back with me, back where he belongs.

He can come here, too, says Pelts. I owe you at least that much, and what am I going to do in this big house without my girls? C'mon, he says. Let me do this. If things work out, you can sell the other place and have some money for yourselves, stay on here … Please, just think about it.

This is your house anyway, Annie. When it went on the market I bought it because you'd lived here all those years. And also the matter of Teddy …

I want to stay. I don't need to think about it. It's a relief, having someone else to love Mum, and I can't walk away from that. The next morning I speak to Joan on the phone, just as I have done at least twice a day, every day. When Mum is settled on the couch, Pelts and I head back to get Grandad.

We go to the house. I pack Grandad's stuff and some more things for Mum. There's nothing else I want for myself. If I had a photo of Teddy I would take that, but it's only now I realise that we don't have any photos. It never mattered until this moment.

When we arrive at the oldies' home, Joan is at the front desk, waiting to greet us. Grandad looks healthy enough, clean and well fed, only I can tell by his eyes that he's had more than a few blowouts and he is quieter overall. It will take some time for him to forgive me although, of course, he doesn't remember that he needs to.

The first day Grandad is a bit disorientated—respite care and then this unfamiliar house and garden, it's all too much. He wets the bed during the night and I spend the morning getting him showered and washing his bedsheets. I stick around after the breakfast is cleaned up because Grandad is pacing from window to window, pushing his face against the glass and peering out, as if the windows were portholes.

Off you go, Shells, says Pelts.

I stammer something about Grandad. He cuts me off: I'll work it out as I go, he says. I imagine that's what you had to do. Everyone needs some time of their own and you've got some catching up to do. I won't be taking no for an answer. He sounds slightly rough and unfamiliar, although he is smiling kindly when I turn to him.

I walk a long while, all the way to the back beach, and then I sit on the shore, sifting coarse sand, sifting everything I know but have no words or pictures for, everything and the blank, dead nothings.

I am better with Grandad here. He loves the mornings and the nights, sitting around and talking. Mostly he listens, yet he comes alive with the listening, like fresh wood on a fire. Sometimes he joins in. Sometimes he is on the money and sometimes he is away with the fairies. Pelts and I take turns to play cards with him while we talk.

It is a mad-hatter's party. Mum doesn't join in the trips down memory lane, although she eats and drinks just a little and she responds to what Pelts says, crying mostly, occasionally smiling, and both together. I hang on to every word that comes out of Pelts's mouth as if he is a cult leader, a sea-god. He makes pictures of a life I can't remember, turning my imaginings into stories.

Grandad interrupts with a story from the war or a tale about the horseraces. He talks as if he is in the moment, as if he can see and touch all the people from the past, as if we are all there and here together. He marches on with his ghosts, thunders home on the straight, as if forty or fifty years is nothing.

I find myself talking too. Pelts asks questions about Mum going downhill, about Grandad losing his marbles, about school and Geoff and the gypsy. He gets me going and I remember things that I would rather forget and there is a forgetting forgiveness in the telling, something like relief.

Sometimes I lose it and laugh at the strange stockpot of our stories, at the strange collection of us. Sometimes I smile and cry together. Mum holds her wineglass up to her mouth as we speak, taking tiny, breathless sips. I don't look at her. I look at Pelts. She doesn't look at me. She looks at Pelts or at her feet, flexing her toes nervously under the blanket.

Chapter Seven

Driftwood

1. Wood floating on a body of water or cast ashore by it.
2. Such wood adapted for use in interior decoration.

Dictionary.com, unabridged

Oh, Shells, when your mum left town I felt washed out with the fucken grief. Dean didn't talk about it. One of our workmates, Paddy, mentioned her on one occasion. It was about four weeks after she left and we were laying the footings for the units at Bluff Road. The radio was on and everyone was working away nice and steady, so I wasn't paying too much attention.

Paddy had his head down, concentrating on the work. He asked Dean if he'd heard from Annie. He said it real casual. Dean took a concrete stump, nearest thing handy, but fuck me, have you seen one of those things?

He came at Paddy from the side, knocked him out, lucky he didn't kill him. For a minute I thought he was dead, on my worksite. I went off my trolley. I told Dean: You get off my building site and never come back. Piss off and don't you dare show your face, any–fucken–place where I'm in charge, ever a–fucken–gain.

I was ropeable, Shells.

I would have taken him back because I had a soft spot for that useless bastard, but I'd told him to go and he only needed to be told once. He was a proud son of a bitch, real proud. He would never crawl back and beg forgiveness. That's why he didn't chase Annie, I reckon, because he wasn't the grovelling type.

Breaks my heart that things went awry. I like that word, awry. I used to say it about the dodgy bits of timber—the warped bits that the bastards would tuck away in the middle of a bundle. Now I say it about everything. Awry.

Annie loved you kids more than she loved Dean, and he put himself in the way of that love: it was a deadly move. That's why things got bent out of shape between Annie and Dean, between Dean and everyone in the end, because he turned into a crooked motherfucker.

Annie came over to bring me some dope. I'd prefer to leave the dope out of the story, but I said I'd tell you the whole truth and it begins there.

Annie was getting the gear from Bullser—Steve Bullrani, young bloke, son of the property developer Bullrani. He was the bloke dishing out the heavy stash. It wasn't local dope. He brought it in from elsewhere.

Bullser was a real entrepreneur. He didn't smoke the shit himself, he just liked to talk the talk with the blokes who did. Bullrani tried too hard, but he was the bloke with the choof, so all the wharfies were on civil terms with him. Somehow, even though he was in the thick of the social scene, he was only ever on the edge of it. I mean we were all a bit awry, but Bullser was a different kettle of strangeness altogether.

Things were coming to an end between Annie and Dean, so she was at my place more and more. I would never touch the smoke if Annie was around, or if I was looking after you guys. Who needs dope when there's Annie?

I liked having you kids around and I was glad Annie wanted to be with me. Dean was utterly useless. That sounds a bit rough, but it's the truth. He was a real fucken sluggard.

Now that's a word—sluggard.

As time went on, Annie told me everything. It killed me to see her with you and Teddy, running around, doing fucken everything while Dean was lucky if he made it to work three days a week, and dead-set useless if he did rock up. Reckons he had chronic back pain. Debatable. Chronic fucken lazy, I reckon, and a liar.

At the start he was good though, in the beginning he was alright. You should remember him like that because later on he was fucked. It was impossible to know when he'd turn, but it was a dead-set certainty that he would. We'd work at a paranoid pace, with the radio turned down so that it was just humming, looking over our shoulders with half an ear out. Half an ear, that's what Paddy ended up with, after the incident with the stump.

Pelts fiddles with his own ear distractedly, tugging at it roughly.

Annie knew that she had to get away from Dean. I loved her too much to argue. I told her every day: You know I love you, Annie, like nothing else.

After Annie left town, Bullser came to me. We were at the Wharfie. We were wasted. He started interrogating me. I thought it was a bit over the top that he was acting all wounded about her leaving. I mean, clearly he was in love with her, we all were, but if Annie wanted him to know where she was going, she'd have told him herself.

I said: I'm not at liberty to say. I stared him down, made him look away first. I wanted the shifty little fucker to know that I knew where Annie was; I knew it all. It was old-fashioned injured pride on my part. Even us old fellas feel it from time to time. I couldn't bear the fact that she'd screwed that slimeball.

We were maggoted. It was well after happy hour. Bullser was looking for his window for confession.

He said: Annie knew that I loved her. She must have. You might think that I treated her like a whore; you have to remember that she was fucking me to get the gear. That's how it was, the first time, and whatever we had later on—well, it was defined by that day.

He was pissed as, slurring, but still fidgety and jittery as ever. He said: It's not a copout. I'm not copping out. It's true. You can't turn back time and I chose a bad time to make a move. After that, I couldn't ask her what she wanted unless that's all it was, pipes for pipe dreams, ghost-ship sex and smashed-up cockleshells.

She never refused me, not outright, he said. A couple of times she pushed me away. She said that it was a bad time for her, well a fruitful time really—a bad time because she was fertile and the risk of pregnancy was really high …

Bullser paused at that point. I was grinding my teeth.

He continued: I was weighing the dope and bagging it up. I didn't say anything because, if you didn't interrupt her, she just kept talking, and it was like a song. She went on for a while about cycles, and peak fertility, and mucus.

By then Bullser was crying, never mind for the bartender and the other blokes watching on. He was blubbering. I gave him nothing. He said: Now I'll never know if she loved me. I'll never know if she knew how much I loved her, how much I love her, I should say, because it doesn't go away. I wasn't prepared, I suppose, and when I saw my chance I jumped right in, without a second thought for her, without a first. I was busy counting my own costs.

Pelts glances over at Mum. Stands. He walks over to her. Gently he sweeps her fringe away and kisses her forehead, once, twice, three times.

He starts talking as he resumes his seat by the fire: I wasn't surprised that he was interested because everyone wanted her … hang on, that makes it sound like we were all sex-bent. I loved Annie. To me she was more than beautiful.

As time went on, I twigged that Annie was fucking Bullser to get the gear. It was unfathomable, un-fucking-fathomable, that she would be interested in him otherwise. He was so uptight and efficient. He'd have been a jerky little fucker in the sack. Sorry, Shells.

My thing with Annie was special. You've gotta believe that. It's true. It was different, our secret, and I loved her, Shells. I didn't want to be jealous. It's not like I owned her and Dean would have been lucky if he could get it up, I reckon. She deserved some loving, that's for sure, and I didn't begrudge her the comfort. That's a shitty word—begrudge.

81

Look—Annie rooted Bullser because her hopeless fuck of a partner couldn't pay for his own dope. I know that's your dad—was—well, as far as we know—the point is, you made me promise to tell the truth and if I make a promise I'll keep it. That's why Annie told me, and me alone, where she was going. That's why she came to me for a bit of comfort, not because she had to.

Bullser was a strange cat. It was like he didn't really want to fit in, not all the way. On the one hand, he tried really hard to be a part of it, and on the other hand he pulled away. He made people feel edgy in his company. He was a dead-set oddball.

Here's an example, right, he'd shout a round for twenty of us, as if he really wanted in, only then he'd say: Catch you later, fellas, like he had somewhere more pressing to be, and he probably did, entrepreneurial fuck that he was.

Bullser talked the talk and he'd have a beer with us sometimes, but he never got out of control. In the real world, and that's where I live, everyone has an off day, when they have too much and lose it with a friend, or an on day, when they're gagging for a good time, when the beer tastes crisp and right and it's gliding down a treat. Everyone overdoes it sometimes, slurring and stumbling, losing it with a mate or eyeing off someone's wife, except Bullrani never did—*never*. He was aloof, friendless, a sober motherfucker and always in control.

Aloof—now that's a word. Right, Shells? You look tired, Chelsea-girl. Shall we call it a night? No? Okay, I'll keep on.

We liked to let our hair down. Bullser was different, a twitchy fucker, real uptight. His shoes were always shiny, long, square shoes. Most of the time he wore a jacket, like he was a businessman. I suppose he was a businessman. He stood out. He wasn't one of us, although neither was Annie, not really.

Bullser was a dog—he pimped her—that's only my opinion, but that's what you want isn't it, my opinion?

Don't judge her, Shells. You have to consider what she was up against. Dean put her in that position and Bullser, the slithery little fucker, he saw his chance and he went for it, hammer and tong.

He wanted Annie to up and away with him to Greece. Annie told me that herself. As if that was going to happen, Shells. Bullser was batting way above his average.

We all loved Annie like she was one of us, even though she was better than all of us put together. I'd like to think I did everything I could, but I loved her like there was a time limit on it. I was scared fuckless I would lose her. That's how it is with angels. Sorry, Chelsea-girl … Give me a second. Sorry …

Pelts takes a long sip of his wine and then refills mine. He bends his head towards his shoulder, wiping his tears on his sleeve as he pours wine into his own glass.

We were all desperate for a piece of her and we all used her up in our way. Pelts bursts out crying as he speaks, his voice high-pitched—that's the bottom of the barrel of the fucken truth.

Right, I'm back. I've got it together. I'm trying to tell it straight, that's all. It's not so easy, so here we go again.

I'll start at the beginning.

Annie brought me over the little parcel of choof. I was suffering with my aching joints and she said: Watch out for that stuff, it's not like regular dope, it's laced with chemicals and other shit. It'll blow your fucken head off.

Actually, she probably didn't say fucken because she was a saint and beautiful—but I'm telling the story and I say fucken like hello, that's the thing, so don't mind me. I'll try to keep it as accurate as I can, as the crow flies and all that.

I only had a crack at Dean's gear because I was having a bad spell with my aching hands. Annie brought me over the gear and she said: Sit down. I'll get you some soup. She was good, a real sweetheart, and I wished I'd never met Dean. I wished I was younger and I had loads of money to offer her. I'd buy her a palace because she was the kind of girl you'd do anything for. Annie and Dean were from different planets. He was an apathetic loser.

According to Dean, Annie had a phobia about marijuana. According to Annie, Dean was choofing it up like there was no tomorrow. He'd suck down the bongs as soon as he walked in the door and then he'd sprawl out on the couch like a fucken carcass. He said: I go to work—who does she reckon pays the bills? He said: Jesus Fuck-a-Duck Christ, so I like a pipe after work, what's the big deal?

He had a habit of doing that, of putting other words in between the ones you expected: Jesus-something-Christ or whatever. He was quick with his tongue, quick-witted I mean, at the start he was anyway. He didn't realise he was clever, or he didn't give a shit.

That's the difference between an after-dinner spliff and a bucket bong (a bucket of bucket bongs in Dean's case). Dean didn't get it. He was off his face all the time. Back then, I was having a quiet joint in the evening. It was a good way to unwind after a really physical day and it helped me sleep. I thought it was better than popping pills at least.

As time went on, Dean wasn't so quick—in fact, he would say the same things, whingeing, negative things, again and again. He changed, whittled away and then there was only anger, ugly fucken anger.

Okay, Shells, here we go again—I promised you the truth. It's fucken awful, all true, and I've every reason to feel guilty.

When you were born, that was the beginning of the end, the last fucken straw. After that I wrote him off, couldn't abide him anymore.

Dean was having a beer at the Wharfie—he was making out like it was a joke, the way you were born. He was calling out to everyone: Charge your glasses—to the miracle baby—born on the kitchen floor. You were born late at night so this would have been the next day.

He was making out like it was something to be proud of—his not even being there—*no one* being there. He was thick as a fucken plank, a dead-set half-wit. That's the closest we ever came to blows.

When he mentioned the placenta, I dragged him to the men's. I held him up against the wall by his throat. He was a skinny little bastard, that's because of the mull, it keeps you trim, explains why I'm a bit of a fat fuck now, ay, 'cause I like my tucker and I wouldn't have a bong these days if you paid me.

Anyway, I held him up by the jugular. I told him if I ever heard him speaking about Annie like that again I would *end* him. A woman having a baby, that's a sacred thing, certainly not for a pub full of stinkin' wharfies.

I couldn't believe Annie was alone for the birth. I was shattered she didn't ring me.

Hang on a minute. Give me a second. It kills me— imagining her all alone in labour …

We sit in silence awhile, taking small sips of wine, breathing deeply. Pelts wanders back over to Mum, holding the glass to her lips. She looks him dead in the eye as she sips, eyes sparkling like diamonds on the bay.

Grandad stands up and paces, up and down the room, back and forth, muttering, as he always does when he's getting sleepy. Pelts wanders over to the wine rack and pulls another bottle, the same gutsy red. He places the bottle next to his chair and grabs the corkscrew from the mantelpiece. He also takes the dominoes and marbles. Here you go, old mate, he says, placing them on the floor beside Grandad's chair. Grandad settles himself on the floor. Pelts knows Grandad's moves now and I watch on gratefully. I catch Mum looking at me. We look away immediately, frightened of ourselves, like infatuated teenagers.

Pelts launches back into his memories.

I don't know what the hell was in the shit that Bullser was dishing out, but it was a far cry from your homegrown variety, a far fucking cry. My hands were aching like a motherfucker, so Dean said he would get me something decent. He said Annie would drop it off at my place on the way to her cleaning job.

When Annie came to my place to drop off the stash, that's when I asked her to get rid of the other job and work for me. It was spur of the moment. Truth is, I'm not so fussy, but I hated to see her so black under the eyes. I asked her if she wouldn't mind telling me what she was getting for the other job and then I matched it, said I needed her to clean my place two nights a week. It suited Annie better because I paid her cash and she didn't have to declare anything.

I pretended I couldn't manage because of the arthritis. It wasn't a hard job. In the end, it was cleaner than I needed it to be and I overpaid her. I liked having her around, turning my house into a home and whatnot.

I was in love with her from the start.

When Annie left town, Dean didn't say a word. He came back to work a week or so later and I stared hard at him, real hard—made sure he knew that I didn't need him, telling me Annie had gone. We were thick, Annie and I, and that's why she gave me the postbox details when she left.

Dean knew that he'd done his dash. Annie would never forgive him and she was a forgiving soul. I've got my own broken relationship and my own river of silence to follow, so I'm not saying anyone's perfect, but he was twisted, right at the heart of himself, like a piece of driftwood, only dead fucken ugly.

See all the driftwood along the mantelpiece? I collected all of that with Annie. I love the way the wood twists in on itself. I love the knots and the holes. I could sit and marvel at that stuff all day, the way the tide has worn it away, whittling down the weak spots so that it looks awry, on the one hand, but perfect, like the essence of itself, on the other.

Annie and I would walk along the back beach, collecting driftwood and shells. We went to the beach when I couldn't bear to watch her work. I said it was good for my arthritis. So many times I've rubbed my hands over that wood and thought about her. I know every curve, every dip …

We had sex a few times, well more than a few. Probably you don't need to know that … I promised to tell you the truth. The first time was just after she started cleaning my place. I bought her a book for her birthday: *Sea Stories*. She didn't take the book home in case Dean went off his head; she'd read it when she was here. I made sure she took some time, put her feet up.

I kept the book all these years because I hoped she'd come back. I never stopped hoping.

Annie said: Only make contact if he's coming after me. She made me promise, she made me swear that if I loved her, I would leave her alone.

The ocean was everything to Annie, life and death. Not a day went by when she didn't go to the water—you would know that. That's where all her little sayings come from. It was always about the sea. You know what I'm talking about: Caught between the devil and the deep sea—that was one of her favourites, and that's why she had to go because it was true. She had too much suffering and we're all to blame in our way.

She said the sea is like God, the God-like sea, it gives and it takes away and you never know when or why, because you can't understand, and I've thought about that a lot, and I think she's absolutely right.

She loved to walk along the shore when the wind was up. She loved to be near the sea when it was windy. She said you can feel your soul in your throat, and it made you want to cry with the knowing, but it wasn't sad—only you suddenly understood some stuff that only God should know. She's the smartest person I've ever known. You know that, of course you know.

Dean was an ugly operator. He threatened Annie. They had a massive blowout. He was a scary bastard, ruthless, no less so on the grounds of love or whatever. He accused Annie of fucking Bullser. He would have known, all along, that Annie was rooting Bullser because he was getting more than he could afford, but something snapped and suddenly he went mental about it. He freaked out, saying Bullser must be Teddy's dad. I thought Teddy was born before Bullser was big in town. The timing's a blur, even for me, and Dean fried his mind, you see.

He said he knew that you were his from the get-go because you were the spitting image of your mum, although he always had his doubts about the boy. The reasoning ... He threatened to deliver Teddy back to his real dad, if Annie would let him know who that might be.

Annie threw a plate at him. Although he dodged, it cut his cheekbone, under his right eye. I thought of her every time I looked at that crooked scar. It looked like a permanent, angry tear—a bruise-coloured tear. He wasn't the crying type of course.

Annie took him on, right in the thick of his rage. Most blokes wouldn't have dreamed of it. She's the gutsiest woman I've ever known. Annie told Dean that if he so much as looked at her children the wrong fucken way, she'd make sure as shit that he would rot in hell. She probably wouldn't have sworn though, so take out the swearing. Then he left and Paddy patched up his cheek, dodgy as—Paddy's a plasterer. That's why it healed so red and angry.

Dean said he would never do anything to hurt Annie. He said: I never woulda done nothin'. Hard to believe that he was a brainy bastard. You should've seen how he used to work out the building calculations, quicker than lightning, faster than any of the guys with proper qualifications. He pissed it against the wall, shitted it to hell, fucken tragedy really.

Everyone was wary of him in the end because he was really snakey, totally un-fucken-reliable, an absolute fire-cracker. I sent him back to the timberyard to collect an order. It had been packed late, allocated for the afternoon run or something. I sent him back mid-morning because it wasn't ready first thing. Three hours later he came back. I shit you not. I rang the Wharfie. When he got back he started kicking the tools around like I owed him the apology.

Anyway, Annie was fed up to the eyeballs with his schizo-phrenic bullshit. She put up with it for a long time, but when he threatened Teddy, well that was it …

After Dean had his eye attended to, he landed at the Wharfie, stayed until close. Then he stumbled back to Marcus's place, pulled an all-nighter, not a wink of sleep in forty hours. The next day he took you, and your brother paddled out in the dinghy. Scared half out of his wits, I'd guess. Poor little bugger.

Apparently, Dean just wanted to give Annie a bit of a fright, but his mind was twisted. He was pissed and bent off his head. Awry doesn't even come close. He drove away with you and not so much as a by-your-leave for the boy. Annie was asleep on the beach, out for the count, because she worked too fucken hard. Teddy was up the beach a short way, looking after you, Shells, giving your mum a break … *Sorry*.

Pelts is crying hard now. He gives in to the crying. We all do.

Annie was never the same after that. Even the sex was different. I know that's not the information you're after:

I guess it's part of the story. It was like she forgot how to feel. She was all cut-up, you see, angry as all fuck. She got really skinny.

Dean thought everyone knew something he didn't know. He thought everyone was rooting Annie. And Teddy was gone, and there's no recovering from that, not for any of us, especially not for Annie.

She loved you kids and the sea. I was part of the mess. I can see that now. In our own way, we were all culpable. We all loved her, Shells, fucked up as that sounds.

Chapter Eight

Starry-eyed

Starry-eyed: Having a naively enthusiastic,
overoptimistic, or romantic view; unrealistic

The American Heritage Dictionary

I'll tell you about my last day with your dad, Shells. It was his
last day on earth as it turns out ...

Most days, I would pop into the Wharfie on my way
home and have a couple of beers after work. The maggot
crowd were always there and they stayed until closing
time. It was mostly old blokes aching for a bit of yesterday,
piss-stained pants and nicotine-stained fingers, but it was a
family for some of them and it wasn't so different from other
families, all in all. They were resolved to the losses, those
blokes. They were caked in loss of one kind or another.

On that last day, Larry pulled up a pew next to me. We
sat at the bar with Dean and Fuller was there, too. 'To
starry-eyed,' said Fuller, and we all raised our glasses and had
a sip because that was his trademark line. Fuller was everyone's best mate, in a way, because he was harmless and he

didn't ask for anything. Dean was a different kettle of fish altogether.

Larry started talking. We knew his stories inside out and back to front. He started to tell the one about the game of cricket that got out of hand (he hit his kid with the bat). He was describing the house in Melbourne, the clinker brick with the buffalo grass like carpet.

Dean was in one of his concrete-stump moods. I could pick it a mile off: squinty eyes, snide comments, twitchy and jumpy and chain-smoking. He said: I thought you were living in Queensland when you had the kids. He said it off the cuff, like: Pass me the smokes, just as if he didn't mean anything by it, but he was ten times smarter than those guys and they knew it. He lorded it over them with his snarly grin.

Larry smashed his pot of beer on the bar and came at Dean. I'll be fucked if he wasn't going to slit his throat. I managed to sit Larry down on a stool. I talked to him in a real even voice about a tip I had on the dogs.

I could hear Dean sniggering in the background and I coulda knocked his block off. I was watching Larry and I was listening for Dean. I was wondering if Larry was gonna have another go. He looked like he was still thinking about it. He was inhaling the cigarette smoke deeply, swallowing a couple of times before blowing it out. He was double-smoking the smoke, chewing on it, wringing every last chemical out of it.

Dean wandered off to play darts and I didn't like the idea of him with any sharp objects in his hand. I kept looking behind. I was jerky and paranoid, swearing, like I had Tourette's or something.

Dean threw the darts, one at a time, biting his bottom lip and concentrating as he launched, laughing as he nailed the bullseye. He was all smart-arse superiority, but his laughter was distracted and I knew him well enough to know that it would end in something ugly.

I made sure Larry was calm. I bought him a coupla shots because it was his kid's birthday: that's why he was going on about the cricket-bat story.

After I'd sorted Larry out, I headed for Dean. Let's take a walk, I said.

I drove Dean back to his place.

Come in for a bit, he said, and I didn't want him heading straight back to the Wharfie, so I obliged.

There was an esky beside his chair, on his right. On the left, there was a bong and a bottle of bourbon. It was ready and waiting for him when he came home, all set out like a welcome-home dinner, without the welcome home, or the dinner, and that clinched it, I suppose, everything he'd become.

Dean pulled out a chair for me and we sat down. Larry got so fucken worked up, he said, knocking the top off a couple of stubbies, all because I put a spanner in the works while he was taking his trip down memory lane. The cricket-bat story was in Queensland, said Dean. He's as thick as a fucken …

It's his kid's birthday today, I said.

Well there you go, said Dean. It's my birthday today, too. You're not gonna let a bloke spend his birthday alone, are ya?

So I settled in and drank his beer. Dean knew what he was playing at with Larry. If the stories changed, there was always a reason. Larry was putting the pieces together so he could sit with his story, or not sit with it, y'know, because that's what they do at the Wharfie, they sift their stories.

Those blokes tell their stories by mood and the mood changes, day to day, so we don't ask questions, not the interrogating kind anyway. We all knew Larry's cricket-bat story like the back of our hand. Dean was being a smart-arse.

The point is—if you can't read the mood, if you're not dead certain that you're on the money, it's best to shut up. Down at the Wharfie, mood is truth. Dean knew that. He knew it better than anyone.

Dean never joined in the Wharfie's storytelling parade. He was a bit of a dark horse, they said, but that's bullshit because we all knew his memory lane, we all knew his ugly truth. Or so we thought …

The thing is: if your regrets aren't the cancerous kind, you can conduct your way through the memories. You can keep some things still and quiet and encourage a bit of noise from the pretty stuff. The problem is that boozers and bongers don't have much of the pretty, so it's all about keeping things still and quiet. That's the starry-eyed that Fuller was always on about, stillness and a bit of quietly goes.

Dean needed more dope and more grog. It wasn't touching the sides. He wasn't getting any distance. The ugly stuff was getting louder. It was gaining momentum and he couldn't get to starry-eyed, no matter how hard he tried, and he gave it a red-hot go. I've never seen anyone try harder.

I said: Larry was having a bad day.

Larry's a cunt, snarled Dean, and I shut up then. You know what he said to me?

I wasn't keen to talk, but Dean insisted that I answer him: *You know what he said to me?*

What? I said.

He said drowning is supposed to be a nice way to die. He said you go into some sort of trance when your brain is deprived of oxygen. He said Teddy wouldn't have felt a thing.

That was years ago, I said. He was trying to cheer you up.

I don't fucken care, said Dean. He pulled a bong and took a good long sip of his beer. He said: Annie belted her fists into my chest. She screamed at me: My Boy. My Boy. My Boy. Of course Teddy felt it, he said. You don't die without feeling it. Larry's as thick as a fucken plank.

Dean had never mentioned Annie to me before. He hadn't breathed a word about her since she left, and no one dared to ask about her, for fear they'd cop a concrete stump in the ear.

Dean said: I held Annie's wrists tight. I pinned her to the lounge. I said: You get your shit together.

I couldn't believe what I was hearing, Shells. I didn't say a word. I was screaming on the inside.

Dean said: Aah, cheer up, Pelts. Thou shalt look at the world through starry eyes. Then he handed me a shot of bourbon.

I was reluctant, I mean I wasn't much of a drinker by then. He was in a mood where you didn't want to leave him alone and you didn't want to cross him. He was chatty and he was never chatty; there was some sort of agenda. I couldn't put my finger on it.

To Fuller, he said, and he downed the bourbon, easy as pie.

Fuller had tattoos of large stars stamped around his eyes, stretching above his eyebrows and across his cheeks. His eyes glistened inside the stars, shiny and dead-wet, like the eyes of a washed-up toadfish. Fuller looked scary, I suppose, but there wasn't a poisonous bone in his body.

Fuller knows how to keep his starry-eyed distance from the memories, said Dean. He's got it down pat.

Fuller was a weathered old fisherman. He spent his days at the Wharfie, watching the waves roll in, breathing roughly through his nose, long and slow. His breathing sounded like the waves, washing on to shore. Dean and Fuller watched their fair share of weather rolling across the bay, smoking their ciggies and drinking their beer, as if they didn't have any part to play in their own lives, as if time were weather. Dean liked Fuller because he didn't ask anything of you. He was empty of bitterness; he was empty full stop.

Fuller wore raggedy old fisherman's clothes, but his shoes were always brand spanking. When he needed new shoes, he went to Kmart in Rosebud. He took off his old shoes and tried a few pairs on. He walked around awhile to check the fit and then he stuffed his old ones back in the box and waltzed out in the pair of choice. He modelled them for us at the Wharfie. He said: Who looks at your shoes?

I think the shoes were important to him because he spent half his life in soggy, old gumboots, out on a boat. I think that's probably why although I never asked him. Like I said: questions were out of bounds at the Wharfie.

Won meself a very decent trifecta today, said Dean. How's the timing? Life's a bad joke, I tell ya. I shouted a round or two for the boys, bought Fuller a meal: bangers and mash, 'cause he's got no teeth. Fucken gummy shark.

Dean went on: He's a legend, Fuller. You gotta love him. I tell him: God I love you, Fuller, and he says: What's not to love? We're a lot alike: world fucked him, too. Fuller always says—Stay starry-eyed, Deano, and I'm on me way now, I reckon, on me star-studded way. If I could wake up and feel like this every day, star-studded and starry-eyed, life coulda been a dream.

He never talked like that, Shells. He was a closed shop. I should've twigged something big was going down.

Dean said: When you least expect it, things shift and by then you're too maggoted to pretend ghosts aren't real.

I said: Dean, what's going on? What are you talking about?

Dean poured us another shot and cracked us another beer. He was having a pipe at each turnover, too, but I didn't smoke anymore. He blew the smoke right at my face. I was sitting directly opposite, and I might as well have pulled the bong myself, the smoke was so thick.

I said: You don't need that shit, Dean.

Dean said: I fucken need it. You better believe I need it. He packed another bong and pulled it in one hit to prove the point. He went on, speaking through the smoke: Annie came home crying. She said that Bullser refused to give her the dope on the house. I told her: You get back there and show him what you got. You give 'im what he wants. As she walked out the door, I called after her: *Don't you be comin' back here without the gear.*

Dean was yelling everything out like he was reliving it. I was definitely a bit stoned, just sitting in the room with him, and we were drinking at a fast pace, too. I couldn't believe what I was hearing. Dean wasn't a talker, you see.

He said: When Annie left I started pulling threads out of that ugly fucken lounge suite. He pointed to the armchair I was sitting on. It looked like it was covered in old schoolroom carpet, grey with a green thread. It's a poor-man's couch, he said, and I sat there and pulled out the slimy green threads, line by line, until she came back. I laid all the threads across that shitty cane coffee table. She took her time coming back, too, like she was enjoying it or something. I was on the couch, watching telly. She laid the choof near the green threads. Watch out for that one, she said, pointing to the little package wrapped in tin foil. Bullser said it's laced, and you need to be careful.

Bullser's a soft-cock greaseball, cunt-pimping maggot, said Dean. He said it without any momentum, like he didn't give a shit. He kept his eyes on the stash; yawned like he'd been having a bit of a doze. Annie reached out to collect the threads.

Leave 'em, Dean said.

Annie said: Why would you do that? She shifted her weight from foot to foot, sighed, stood still a moment or two, and then moved to sit down.

You reek, said Dean. Go have a shower.

It's impossible to believe how horrible he was. I couldn't believe he was sitting there in front of me, Shells, reliving his horribleness, making me relive it. I was dying inside. I die inside every day, Annie-girl, because I should have done more.

Dean said: I ripped into the gear as soon as I heard the water running. I went straight for the potent one and I didn't mix it with tobacco. I was concentratin' hard on the rush. I was staring hard at the green threads and kiddin' myself that I deserved something better than a poor-person's couch. I was off me tits by the time she came back out, off me fucken head. I ghosted me misdemeanours right out of the house.

It was bourbon, beer and then bong. Again and again. That's all he did, Shells. I was feeling like I might vomit, but he kept going. I was starting to worry that he was going to kill me. I was stoned. Just by virtue of sitting in the room, I was off my head and paranoid.

Dean said: While she was in the shower I got up and collected her things from outside the bathroom door. I heard her vomiting in the shower and I took her things back to the couch. When she'd finished, I was on the couch with her undies in my hand and a couple of the stray green threads.

Dean went on: She stood in the doorway, towelling her hair. I held her undies up to my nose and breathed them in: her and the seaweed threads and all the poor-man's wrongness. She lunged forward and tried to take her undies. She was wet, dripping on my lips, my eyelids. She had a towel wrapped around her. We both pulled and I could hear a ripping noise as the stitching came undone. I was breathing her sweaty smell, and then there was the freshly washed smell of her, too, so sweet. It was all mixed together, sweat and soapy-clean skin.

I wanted him to stop, Shells. He talked and talked, on and on.

He said: I decided I wasn't going to let go first. Then I changed my mind, simple as that, and quick as lightning I let go. It was fast and she fell back awkwardly, thumping against the floorboards, nursing her wrist because she landed so hard, and then collecting her towel because she was all wet and spreadeagled.

I laughed. It was only the fall I was laughing at, the random clumsy stumbling. There was nothing funny, only the smoke had set in and I was getting some distance.

She made it to her feet, crying, wiping her tears on her stretched-out undies. Then she held her undies tight, clenched in her good hand. She held them so tight that I couldn't see the pink of them anymore and the room became blank and starry.

Her blue eyes were like ice when she was cut up like that, like angry ice, struck with lightning shards. I turned to the telly and she left me to my laughing. It was a windy day and the aluminium venetians rattled along, echoing my tinny laughter.

Oh God, Shells, says Pelts, his head in his hands, knuckles pounding his forehead. I was crying, fists clenched, breathing hard out of my nose. Dean didn't care. It was like he couldn't see me. He just kept talking, on and on.

Dean said: Annie yelled at me. She said: You're the pimping cunt. I never heard her say cunt, only that once, and now I wonder if I imagined it. I wonder if I made it up, re-remembered the memory. Distance is a shifty bastard, he added. Memory is a motherfucker of a game.

I'd never seen him so wasted, Shells. There was something else going on because he was a seasoned drinker and he'd bonged half his life away. I should have worked out what was happening.

Dean said: I never gave a fuck about anything 'cept making sure I stayed wasted. For a long while it gave me some lead time. Then the distance started to murky up and fucken change.

I told him: That's why Larry messed up his story.

I know, said Dean. You think I don't know how things start to ghost up the spaces if you're not on your guard? I lost Titch in all that, he said, on top of everything else. He was the best dog ever. A pure heart.

I said: It was a long time ago, Dean. I wanted him to shut up. I mean, we all played our part, getting Teddy out of that morgue. Me and Bullser—fifteen thousand each. Bullser stood at my door in his shiny shoes and his pressed shirt as if it was a business deal, legitimate and professional. It was guilt money. He didn't take part after that.

Dean was hands-on—I think that on some level he was scared of Annie, her clear goodness frightened him.

Pelts looks over at Mum. She bows her head, chin on chest, closes her eyes. She motions with her hands for Pelts to keep talking. It looks as though she's conducting music. She opens her eyes. Motions again. When Pelts resumes the story, she closes her eyes once more.

Pelts continues—Annie put the hard word on us. You owe me, she said. You will bring Teddy home so I can bury him here, with me, near the water.

Tony worked at the morgue. He was the key to our scamming, the only way we could get it done. Dean threatened Tony. Dean was a ruthless motherfucker and everyone knew it. Tony needed the money really badly, poor bastard. Dean knew it. I knew it.

Tony worked nights at the morgue so he could be with his wife during the day. She was on a disability pension since the neck injury, because of the headaches. The younger kid jumped on her neck. She was sitting down, bent forward to pick up a cup of tea, and the kid took a flying leap off the table. It was a huge blow to the back of her neck. Apparently, the kid is autistic. He throws stuff at her sometimes. Furniture. Food. He doesn't understand why she's lolling about in bed.

Tony was on carer's pension so he shouldn't have been working nights at the morgue on top of that. Dean said he'd dob him in to Centrelink. He said there were ramifications for Bullser, too, because the morgue was his family's business. Bullrani Funerals. Respectful Care for your Loved Ones—what a joke.

Dean said he'd tell all the fellas at the Wharfie that Tony had been getting it off with the dead bodies, even the men. The story fits, Dean told him. You can't be getting much from your wife. That was the clincher, I suppose. Tony was devoted to his family, pure and loving. Integrity was everything to him. It's all he had after all.

Tony agreed to release Teddy's body; he agreed with a nod, tears rolling down his cheeks. It was awful, fucken dreadful. I was there. I'm responsible, too. Tony needed the money. We took advantage.

Everything had already been signed off: death certificate, funeral director's certificate. We opted for cremation. I paid for it. The night before that was due to happen, Dean swapped boy for dog. I didn't know what was in the bag.

Dean said: I loved that fucken dog. See that red glass bottle up there. That's Titch's ashes. He was like a dog version of

Fuller. Loyal, sparkly cunts—the both of them. For his last supper, I gave him scotch fillet. Then I covered his eyes and shot him under the gullet, blew his brains out.

As for the boy, he never took his eyes off me. Paddled out furiously. Dean pulled another bong. The last thing the boy got was my raised fist. I had Chelsea in my arms. Quick as lightning I grabbed her, and the boy moved towards me, with his arms out to take Chelsea. I put my finger to my lips so he knew not to make a sound. Then I raised my fist slowly, slowly and stopped a breath short of his eye. I showed him in slow motion how it would be if I smacked him out. I pointed to the dinghy and he started paddling, barely took his eyes off me. If he looked up I raised my fist again and pointed to the deep blue, so he kept going. I sat on the rock wall with Chelsea until he'd paddled right out. Then I left.

There's no starry-eyed for that. Dean laughed an ugly laugh. It was deep, shot with angry regret. Teddy went out too far. Stupid bugger. I never woulda hurt him.

After that I shut up, says Pelts. I was frightened for my life. I was paranoid, stoned off my head. His lounge room was a hashish steam chamber. I imagined the cops were going to ask questions, all these years later. I imagined them, making demands about the body. I was reliving the night of the switch, the morning of the cremation. I was freaking out all over again that someone would open the coffin. There was another fifteen thousand for Tony if he made sure that didn't happen.

In my mind I was back there all over again. This time around, I imagined that someone ordered a *stop* based on the smell of burning, hairy dog. I don't know how these things work, where the smells go. I was imagining they'd stop halfway because of the rancid, roasted dog smell—or call the cops on account of the canine bones. I was freaking out, that the cops were on their way. I thought I heard sirens. I thought Dean was going to kill me.

I needn't have worried. Dean was struggling to light his own bong and our crimes were buried with Teddy. Well, not really, I mean look at your beautiful mum ...

Are you awake, Annie? You still with us, Annie-girl?

The distance was all close and shady for Dean. He was losing his hold. I should have known.

Dean said: Annie pounded her fists on my chest. She said: The wind will change. You wait and see. You'll hear it first, only you won't be listening. Watch the water if you don't believe me. The wind will change.

Dean said to her: Teddy's dead. Get it together. He had her wrists pinned so she couldn't move. Your boy's not comin' back, Dean said. You get some fucken distance.

Annie spat in his face. Good for you, Annie-girl.

Dean tried to imitate Annie's spitting, but all he could muster was some frothy dribble down his chin. He downed a shot, packed another bong.

Dean said: Now I understand what she tried to say to me ... Caught between the devil and the deep ... Stop. SSSHH. Listen ... Something from the venetians? He was giggling. It was sickening. Stoned-loser-maggot giggling. He was off his head.

Listen, he said again. No-no, it's just the shifting distance.

He was banging down the pills every time he had a shot. He emptied two pill bottles.

Been saving these for a rainy day, he said.

I should have known. I've asked myself if I did know: if I let him go ahead anyway. First he said they were sleeping pills; then he said they were anti-anxiety. Either way he was banging them down like lollies. I was there. I'm accountable.

Larry and Boner found him after a couple of days. They headed to the Wharfie to break the news to Fuller and the rest of us. Before they could say a word, Fuller said: Deano's done and dusted, like he was telepathic or something.

In the end, I had to open Dean's beer for him. I had to pour the last round of shots, pack his bong, because he couldn't manage. It's the last thing I'll ever ask of ya, Dean said. It took him a few tries to get through that last pipe.

Dean said: Annie asked me to come home. She came down the Wharfie and said: *Please* come home soon. I didn't go home right away, of course, and by the time I got home, the baby was born. She didn't have any clothes on and they were all bloodied up, the two of 'em, so at first I thought someone was dead. The blood was only from the birth, of course.

It was like an old movie, he said, before hospitals, and I couldn't believe it and I stood at the end of the bed and watched them sleeping. I realised about the baby because of the blood, the rubbery cord and shit all over the kitchen floor. I nearly stepped in it, that's why I twigged, otherwise I woulda flaked out on the poor-man's couch, none the wiser.

I stood and watched them, he went on, listening to me own jagged breathing, frightened she'd wake up and say it was over between us. Then she opened her eyes and said: Come and look at her, she's beautiful. And that should have been the moment. That should have been me epiphany, to turn me life the fuck around.

Pelts says: I was off my rocker just sitting in the room. I held the bong and he sucked it down hard. The smoke poured out of his nose and mouth, real thick, like he was on fire inside his head.

He was as giddy as all fuck and he wasn't usually like that. He was removed from his own body, looking at his hands, holding them in front of his eyes and then further away. Then he'd look up at me and talk and talk, although I don't think he could see me. He was talking to himself. He was so slurry, sleepy, really hard to understand, but I wasn't asking him to repeat anything, that's for sure.

He tried to stand; his legs were wobbling all over the place.

The distance is getting louder, said Dean. It's all close and sweaty, like her smell in my face …

Dean said: I'm desperate to piss, like I could piss out a whole ocean.

He couldn't walk so I helped him to the toilet. He was laughing, swaying over the toilet bowl. He said: I'm fit to burst. I can't make meself go. Me muscles aren't working. I can't feel below me waist. Seems like you die from the waist down.

Obviously, that was more than a clue and I should have taken him to the hospital. He was completely maggoted. He lost his balance, smacked his head against the toilet bowl and landed on the floor. He was still and quiet for a time, I'm not sure how long, and then he started laughing; the laughter was long and moaning, like wailing. I shook him upright, took him back to his chair.

He said: I'm warm, like I'm in the bath. This must be dying, this warm-bath feeling—he'd wet his pants, that's all, and that's when I left. I got up and drove home. I shouldn't have been driving.

I washed my shot glass and put it away, like I was removing the evidence. I must have known, deep down I must have.

Dean said: Everything's still now, like after the baby girl came. Listen, he said. Look ... everything's sparkly. This is the last thing I'll ever see, me body and me house all lit up and sparkly, and no one to give a shit about me ... That's me own starry-eyed fault of course.

Just before I closed the door, he said: Listen! He was giggling. He was looking at his hands, wriggling his fingers and staring at his hands ... Stop. Look, he said, pointing to the window. Something from the venetians?

Chapter Nine

Bygones

Bygone—past events to be put aside;
'let bygones be bygones' water under the bridge

Based on WordNet 3.0, Farlex clipart collection

We don't know what to do when Mum starts talking. There's no fanfare. No warning. She starts talking and we do not dare to interrupt. She launches in and we are suddenly there with her, in another time. She speaks the memories in present tense as if she's living them again. I see her world in real time and I understand grey, eyes full of grey. I thought I understood before. Now I see.

Charge your glasses, ladies. It's time for the sex quiz. Gen says it like a glitzy compere from the telly and I start panicking. I don't want to play. These girls are my oldest friends but I haven't seen them for years. They're bygone like my dreams.

I excuse myself and nick off to the toilet. Relax, I tell myself. Just play the game. I'm freaking out that I'll unravel and they'll find out all the shabby details of my life. Stay calm, I tell myself. They don't know anything.

We are here for Kel's hens' party. Jill nagged me to come; she wouldn't let up.

I'm edgy about the sex quiz. What will I say? For me, sex is a routine: it's like brushing my teeth. I fuck shitheads and wish they weren't shitheads. I fuck them because I know they're shitheads and shitheads are what I know. I hope, at least, they'll be a good, hard root.

I fuck them like there's no tomorrow, like they're all I've ever wanted, so they'll remember me like I'm their first and only. They'll remember me alright because, for a spell, I'm too good to be true. Putting out like there's no tomorrow, I'm a dream come true.

Stand up if you've taken it up the arse. Gen sits with her glasses poised on the end of her nose, holding the page of questions in one hand and a pen in the other. There's mixed laughter around the table. I ash my ciggie, wait to see who's going to stand. Half the girls around the table rise out of their chairs, five out of ten women, so I stand too.

We're not girls anymore. The wear and tear is beginning to show, especially around the eyes and the forehead. You can tell who has time and money for a bit of pampering.

Interesting odds, says Debbie, scanning the table. I thought it would be higher than fifty per cent, with all you young ones.

I don't know Debbie: husky voice, enormous boobs. I imagine I might have been a bit like her if my life had been happier. Her wrinkles are all smile lines, silver fireworks at the edges of her eyes, the corners of her mouth. I'm glad these other women are here, too, Kel's friends from her new life, otherwise I wouldn't be able to breathe.

I tell myself to relax. It's just a game, all for a laugh. It's surface stuff, doesn't mean I have to tell them how things really are.

Someone has to tell the tale, that's the rule. If no one offers to tell, we vote. Gen scans the table, peering at us over the top of her metallic-mauve glasses.

There's no need to vote. Kel starts telling. That's all he wanted to do, she said. It was all he could talk about at dinner, checking if I'd baulk at it. I nodded along like he was talking about the wine, like I'd done it a million times. She laughs. He was hot—buffed. Makes you wonder though; I might have been a fella for the interest he showed in anything else. She sips her champagne slowly, adjusts her glasses. He had really bad breath, she says with a laugh, so it was a relief not to be face to face.

My memory shifts to the grime of my life, to the repeated struggle to start each day fresh, knowing all the while that it's the same old, same old—I wouldn't care so much but for my precious children. They deserve better than a second-hand life—a deadbeat drug-pig dad.

I'm a cleaner. It's hard, physical labour: floors and bathrooms, bending and sweating, making things look new and sparkly, kidding myself that there's something lasting, something good. My body is in pretty good shape. I'm strong, skinny and tanned. I love a bit of sun. My exercise is my work because my life is non-recreational. I love a ciggie, but I'm not weathered by it. I look healthy enough on the outside.

I have a few lines on my forehead, around my eyes and mouth, like smile lines except they're from the disappointment.

Kel starts talking about the good old days: blue-light discos and long, lazy afternoons at the beach, dusting off the sand to paint each other's toenails. She jumps from story to story but ties it all together somehow. I have no idea how she remembers. In my world the past is over—you don't dredge it up. Kel is openly emotional. Of course she is: her secrets are clean and she wears them on her sleeve. She lets it all hang out and everyone loves her. Who else would have got us all back together for the sake of a wedding?

I haven't seen these girls for years. I worked hard to disappear.

Jill is in my face straight away. She reaches for my arm with her soft hands, shiny fingernails, blue-grey. She asks about my life. She wants to know if I'm happy, centred. She can't even wait until I have a few drinks on board. Jill was my best friend in the old days, when the world was awash with sparkly dreams.

I don't know what was I thinking. She looks corporate, affluent: lacy black camisole under a sheer blouse, unbuttoned at the neck to accentuate the bronze knuckles of her lean collarbone. I'm wearing jeans and thongs. Jill said 'casual'. She said we'd order Thai food to come to us. They're lipsticked and blow-waved as if today is the wedding.

Tell me about your family, Annie, she says.

Sure, I say. I'll just nick to the toilet.

As if I'm going to tell Miss Perfect Life about drug-fucked Dean, doped up to the eyeballs and useless—how to describe my clear-shiny children: silky blonde, pink cheeks, pinker lips … I long for them. I don't owe Jill answers. Our friendship is as withered as my dreams.

I head back out to the living area and beyond it, the balcony. I lean over the railing, staring at the still water, only a few ripples, yearning for my stretch of beach—not so far along. I light a ciggie and think of my people. I imagine these old school friends with my new crowd. My beach people are rough around the edges, but they don't miss a trick. They know that good mothering is a breath away from death.

Gen says: Stand up if you've had intimate sexual relations with another woman, even a kiss?

I laugh on cue, stay busy with my ciggie. A few of the girls stand. Renee asks Kel if she's standing because of the time she pashed Emily; that was a scandal when we were fifteen. Emily is a full-blown lezzo now, apparently.

She was a great kisser, says Kel, shrugging it off and laughing, so happy in her own skin that nothing can touch her and everyone wants to. The girls get talking about Emily: long bronze legs, blonde hair, sickeningly straight and shiny, all the guys were dying for her. We wonder about it a moment or so, laugh about what's become of us all. I put out a laugh. It comes back like an echo. That's what bygone is, after all, a claustrophobic echo.

Kel tops up the drinks. She asks Jill about her silky shirt: designer … availability … I miss my beach people. There's no interrogation where I'm from: no talk of boutique labels with secret pronunciations. We shop at Kmart or the op-shop: a shirt's a shirt. The tide washes in and we forget about yesterday. It's the land of no regrets and we take it for granted that we're all running away from something.

I ran away from my family. I was sixteen. It was summertime, tourist time, plenty of work around. After a few years, I had Teddy and later, Chelsea. When Teddy was born, I rang home. I was going to tell Dad about my new baby boy, Teddy, named after him. Mum answered and she launched in before I could say anything. She said: Your brother is dead. I could hear wet static, crying and spitting through clenched teeth. You have destroyed this family because you wouldn't let it be *bygone*. The midwife was in the room so I made out like I got the answering machine. I stammered something about calling back later and I hung up. That's the last time I cried for echoes.

I'll make you a cup of tea, said the midwife. It's overwhelming, this wee baby and the rush of hormones. Have a cup of tea, lovey, and I'll help you with a shower ... Where are your people at, lovey? She spoke offhandedly as she took my blood pressure, eyebrow cocked—I pawed Teddy's soft cheek and wallowed in the hiss of deflating air.

I ditched the shiftwork after Teddy was born. I put a sign in the window of the grocery store: House Cleaning. Reasonable Rates. I figured I was cleaning up my life. There are degrees of cleanliness, of course, depends how you look at it. But don't worry about the grime; there is always the tide. That is the paradise of the seaside: bygones, washed away.

When I clean the beach houses, I usually take the children along. I watch Teddy jump on their trampolines and ride their bikes. I park Chelsea's pusher near a pretty window, overlooking the garden. I sip imported tea and watch Teddy play outside. For a fleeting moment, it's like being on a holiday.

Then the bygones come haunting—it's all dust and family bitterness, bathroom scum and scoured opportunities. I work double time, sweating and puffing, harder, faster, until I'm too fucked to think, light-headed from the bleach.

On the way home, I lean down and kiss Teddy on the head. Chelsea sleeps soundly in the trashy tartan pusher and I pull the purple fleece blanket around her dear little forehead. I pretend the beach is just a phase and soon I'll go to a happier seaside, a leisure-time beachfront with choices where I really belong. Only I belong here of course because, in my world, belonging is surviving.

My beach people don't give a flying fuck about your problems, or if they do, they have too much on their own plate to worry about it. But don't kid yourself that they don't know—they know.

My beach people lack the shifts of emotion that wash across the lucky people's faces. Their expressions disappear before you can read them, coming and going like ripples on the water.

At the beach, we bury our regrets and that's that—we dig them under the sand or throw them to the gulls—the tide washes in and out and there's no trace. At the beach, everyone just wants to move on. There's no time for dreams. Intimacy is not a choice here; it's gritty—survival and necessity.

C'mon, doll, give us a smile, eh. Put on some lippy and a nice pair a' shoes. Good as new; there y'are, doll. I've got some powder will cover that. Take a couple of these anti-inflammatory numbers, wash 'em down with your wine, a good long sip. There y'are. See? Now have a fag, it'll help with the breathing, nice and slow, in and out. Men are cunts, doll.

If the tide takes too long to wash in, we turn to the grog. Alcohol is the root of all evil and all that. Cheers! That's our seaside sense of humour. We laugh whenever we can and nothing lasts until tomorrow. Nothing is all that funny, but we laugh a lot and tomorrow has no memory.

I don't get to the pub much anymore because I have the children; these days I don't really see anyone. I miss the laughs because empty laughing is better than nothing. I just go cleaning or potter around at home with the children, thinking about all the things I want to give them. If I didn't love them and I didn't know them and I didn't need them, I should have got rid of them. But I was afraid. Abortions make the silence so thick.

Jill passes her wallet around, bursting with snaps of her shiny, happy family, yanking me back into the moment. I have a quick look and murmur approvingly. I take a closer look. I've seen her husband before. I know him …

Jill doesn't look as though she's had one baby, let alone two. That's what you get when life is just for pleasure: off to the gym and then a facial, top it off with a low-carb lunch and a skinny soy latte, perhaps a massage. Jill probably has someone like me cleaning her house and then someone else (with a better education and more reputable qualifications) to look after the children. I excuse myself, head back to the toilet.

I sit there awhile: resting my head against the cool, clean, white wall. I shouldn't have come. Jill insisted; she called and called. I didn't respond to her messages. Eventually, she teamed forces with Fran: calling from Fran's phone. I thought it was about the cleaning …

In the end I gave in—I had forgotten how seductive it is to be wanted. I'll sneak away soon; I'll make an excuse about the children: Teddy has hurt himself or Chelsea is sick. I can walk home from here. It'll take the best part of an hour, but walking alone is a luxury and walking alone with the wash of the waves at my feet—utterly orgasmic, all for me.

I never leave my children. Dean doesn't watch them properly—dead-dog, comatose cunt. I want to be home with my babies, soaping their delicious necks, tucking them up in warm, clean pyjamas. Why did I come?

I grab another stubbie on my way back out to the table, hoping the sexual quiz is over soon. Actually, I hope it goes on all night because it blanks out the opportunity for any real conversation. I down half the beer, accept a glass of wine. Line 'em up, girls, that's the way, so I can numb the fuck up. Where I come from, no one needs to know too much and I have my aloneness. No one minds me and that's the way I like it.

Gen says: Stand up if you've done quirky sex, bondage, cross-dressing, anything outside the square?

Jill stares at me. I don't stand up. She knows I'm lying; she can always tell. Maybe I should tell the truth. I've done bondage, whoop-de-do. Tie me up and hurt me, get off on your own power, grip my windpipe so you can make me come harder—what do I care? It's skin level.

The real truth: I'm a slave to every ugly mistake I've made and I make them again and again, every day. Sometimes a mistake is the best I can do, that's bondage, shackles are nothing. At least I choose (who I screw, when I come). I'm a fabulous pretender. You'll think I've come like a steam train. Truth is I can hold off for hours. Coming is a state of mind and I avoid the intimacy. I prefer to come alone, panting longingly under the stars ... only the wash of the sea for company.

Gen says: C'mon, girls, surprising me and standing. You can't tell me that no one else ...

Sarah stands. He was a strange bird, that's all I'm saying. A bad egg, she says.

Jill is staring at me. Everyone is staring at me. Are they staring at me because I'm going red, or am I going red because they're staring at me? I stand because the 'bad egg' threw me. I'm a great liar, a professional, but today I'm tripping myself up and I can't get the air in. I stand, sucking the smoke down hard. I look up at the sky and exhale, blowing the smoke up and away at the stars. It's a clear night, clear as a bell, whatever that means.

I wander over to the edge of the verandah and watch the moon on the water. I wonder if the view would look the same if my life were different.

Someone has to tell, says Gen. I choose Annie.

Why me for this one? I don't say anything, but then the vote comes in and I'm on. I'm busting, I say, shifting my weight from foot to foot like I really need to go.

C'mon, Annie. I told my secrets, says Kel.

Yeah, c'mon, says Renee.

The girls are all staring at me—waiting, waiting. My voice becomes a whisper. I was thinking of something else, I stutter, somewhere else …

(Bad egg. Bad egg.)

When my brother was mean to me, that's what Dad would say: He's a bad egg, Annie, an absolute arsehole. Mum said: He's outside the square, that's all, and for years I thought that inside the square were all the nice people, the normal people, and outside the square were all the bad eggs.

I should tell a bondage story—I have a selection. It's mind over matter, mostly, and I couldn't give a fuck if the whole world knows. Tie me up with my legs wide, film it if you want, I couldn't care less … And that's when I remember Jill's husband: Mr Cash. Does she know? Is that why she lured me here, why she wouldn't take no for an answer?

Jill is staring me down. I look at my hands momentarily and draw desperately on my cigarette. I need a way out. I rest the ciggie in the ashtray, run back to the toilet.

Why did I stand for that one? Because I thought they could see that I was lying. How could they have seen? They couldn't have, they're drowning in the reality of their own dreams. I sit on the closed lid of the toilet, my head in my hands, breathing too quickly. I look down at the dusty skirting boards. I'd be more comfortable with a bucket of hot suds and some rubber gloves. I check the cornices, a flossy web in the rear corner. Only a cleaner looks up when they're seated on a toilet.

The paranoia is making me act out of my own skin and nothing seems real. I stay there on the toilet, off my head with the panic, dreading exposure. When I go out they'll want more. You can't rewind time with these people. They hang on to everything with their clear heads and their untangled consciences, fossicking through other people's mess like preened seagulls. They don't understand bygones.

When the bad egg appeared at the bathroom door, I was wearing my shitty old pyjamas and my saggy, bleach-blotched undies. The bathroom and the toilet were my responsibility when I lived at home. I always cleaned them on Saturday mornings.

He is my biggest secret. I keep him at the front of my mind so I remember that I can never tell anyone about him. With these old friends I feel like I am wearing my secrets on my sleeve, except that I'm sleeveless so they're crawling on my skin. Under.

I didn't hear him come in. I was cleaning the shower, the water was trickling and I was scrubbing. I'm nearly done, I said nervously, catching sight of him perched in the doorway, all arms and legs and a small head, like a spider. I have a boyfriend, I said desperately as he was unzipping.

You don't have a boyfriend, he said, smirking. His left eye twitched. It always twitched when he was about to do something mean.

I was reeling in bleach and shock, coughing and spluttering. I knew that he wasn't right in the head, but I never imagined ... I should have been ready ... Strong hands. I wasn't prepared ... fists like steel clamps.

He was rough—brutal—there's your S and M. He left without saying a word. I used my old undies to clean myself up. Bleach, bleach, burning bleach.

I couldn't believe it. Neither could Mum. She said it never happened. She organised the abortion and she said it never happened. A year later, I moved out. I up and left in the middle of the day. It might seem like a sideways move, but it was more of a diagonal. I choose—who I fuck, when I come. My rules—nothing sideways about that.

I flush the toilet and take a few deep breaths, in through the nose, out through the mouth, preparing to face the girls. When I get out there, Jill is in the far corner of the verandah, stooped over the railing, talking quietly to Fran. They're tight those two, with their middle-class blouses and casual diamonds. Fran didn't really hang out with us at school. I thought she was boring. We all thought she was boring.

They come back to the table and I light a fresh ciggie. I don't smoke or drink much these days and I feel giddy-sick, my mouth watering. The conversation has become stilted.

Everyone is pretty pissed now (except Debbie because she's pregnant). The fun has splintered into sharp edges and bitterness. I'm reeling in the sound delay of my own words, echo of echoes, thick thoughts reverberating.

Spill the beans, Annie, says Jill.

It was nothing, I say, racking my mind full of ugly truths, trying to sift something believable and normal out of the wrongness, haunted by his busy limbs like a spider's legs, the pinned-down pinching, shoulders and biceps burning. It was when I f-first moved down here, I say.

I can't think straight. I'm stuttering, speaking too fast. I'm red in the face and I don't know what I'm going to say next. I know I have to keep talking because everyone is quiet, listening, waiting. Kel is giggling all the while, but she's off her face. She knocked back half a dozen stubbies before we arrived, and that was hours ago now.

C'mon, Annie, says Jill.

He was dressed ... like a spider, I blurt.

What am I doing? I should have made it all lies. Now I've snookered myself, putting lies next to the truth, and I feel like a dodgy drama student. I'm not pulling it off and everyone is watching me. I laugh, but it cracks awkwardly as if I'm going to cry.

I remember the shower tiles against my cheek, cold and smooth-wet. I inhale: fire bleach. I exhale: spidery fur-balls catch in my windpipe, wheezing at the back of my throat.

The floor was wet. I slipped over, I say.

Slipped where? says Fran. At school she was boring, a nervous Nelly. She would never have asked me a direct question. Now she's a nosy, pompous lawyer fuck. I could give her the heads-up about sex and everything that goes

121

with it. We think we're all so different, but once you take off the suit and the watch, and wriggle out of the expensive undies, it's all a muchness. I'm tempted to tell Fran to stop interrogating me and ask her husband about his escapades with the Labour Day boys. Same goes for Jill …

Perhaps I should tell them the truth. I'm a cleaner, sometimes there's sex as well. It's easy money and honest enough, from my end anyway. It's not hard. Triple the money for a quick screw, same for a blow.

If there's going to be sex, the wife and kids are back in town and the man is waiting when I come to clean the beach house. That's generally the way of it I've found, more or less—I had no idea. The man loiters around and expectation lurks in the air like his wife's perfume, soft floral, stifling.

It's not hard to manage. Teddy knows not to come inside when I am cleaning the floors so I tell him I'm starting on the floors as soon as Chelsea is asleep—it doesn't take long. It's over soon enough.

The money is steady if you know how to read people and, like I said, I know how to fuck like there's no tomorrow, like there's only tomorrow. If I don't like them, I don't go back. Let them explain to their silky-skinned wives why there's been a fallout with the cleaning lady.

Jill eyeballs me. I hold her gaze momentarily.

Sex has nothing to do with class. Once you're in the thick of it, you can be anyone. The power is in the act. The expensive aftershave gets riddled with good hard-working sweat and there's nowhere to hide, except in your mind. No one gives a shit about your limp six-figure package.

Slipped where? Fran drills me like I'm in the courtroom, under oath, her witness.

Oh ... over the scales, I say. I banged my head, lost consciousness for a second.

You poor darling, says Deb. That's an awful story. What happened when you came to? Did you need stitches?

No–no. It was nothing. Just a ... bad egg.

What do you mean? says Jill.

I mean ... I stand, grabbing hold of my phone and cardigan, readying myself to leave. I hold the edge of the chair to steady myself. Never mind, I say. It's bygone.

Chapter Ten

Mercy

At the mercy of—without any protection against;
helpless before: drifting in an open boat, at the mercy of
the elements

American Heritage Dictionary

I pretend today is any old day, but it's not—I know the baby
is coming.

I take Teddy to the beach in the afternoon—his last day
as an only child. I watch him run away from the waves,
laughing delightedly at the undertow, sparkly wet skin. I
wonder whether I can love another child as much as I love
Teddy. Is there room for all that love? Do I have enough?

I drop by the Wharfie after the beach. I ask Dean if he
would *please* come home early today. I have never asked him
that before. Not once. I don't explain. Dean's friend with the
tattoo eyes like large black stars is staring hard—at my belly,
at my hands, lingering at my breasts. I clench Teddy's hand
and get out of there as fast as I can.

I give Teddy his dinner. He is bleary-eyed and I run him
a bath while he eats. Before long, he is tucked up in bed and

I kiss his soapy-clean neck; his skin smells as familiar as my own. I take the clothes from the line, pausing intermittently in the hazy twilight, crouching—hands flat against the grey concrete path.

Never mind, I tell myself—women have managed this by themselves for centuries, but it's no consolation because those women had each other. I want my mum, even though I haven't seen her for years and I hate her with all my heart.

I take the clothes inside. The wind wheezes in the old roof like a boiling kettle, whirling and tumbling as if it will lift the ragged asbestos at any moment. Nothing would surprise me now. I'm not even here, not really. The aluminium venetians rattle and chatter. I make a cup of tea—in that time, the pain doubles. My belly clenches furiously. A boulder pounds my cervix. I walk to the table, planting my hands there, watching my knuckles turn moon-white as the pain peaks.

I close my eyes. All I hear is the screeching windvane. The force is suffocating—slamming my baby's head down, belting my cervix. I can't make it stop and I cry in harmony with the rusty squeal of the windvane.

I walk the few steps to the iron, collapsing onto one knee as I bend towards the power switch. Shuffling back to the table, I plant my palms against the surface, pushing against the weathered timber as if I am shifting heavy furniture, marching my feet against the floor. I am unsteady. It feels as though my legs are dipping below the floor level. I'm seeing stars.

After five minutes and three long pains I fall, knees and elbows thwacking floorboards. I lay my cheek against the cool boards, surrendering. I vomit but it's clear, only water. I can't even lift my head. The vomit runs along the grooves in the weathered boards—time moves forward in heaving waves.

I pull a towel from the washing basket, resting my head there, closing my eyes. My cheeks are burning; my feet are freezing. I'm so thirsty. The cold, outside smell of the towel is overwhelming and for a moment, I wonder if I'm still outside near the clothesline. Am I dreaming? I see wayward ghosts, flying around the line in the windy tangle of our clothes. Familiar ghosts, dancing in our clothes. I open one eye—I'm on the kitchen floor. I'm losing it—mind and body separated—this is what labour does. No need for drugs. I'm elsewhere.

Pushing my underwear over my ankles, thighs aching, calf muscles cramping. My movements are spasmodic and I accidentally move the towel that is under my head. Crying wildly, I push up onto my hands and knees, growling—I no longer sound like me.

The height of my body from the floor dizzies me. Dry-retching, I lower onto one elbow, trying to reach inside myself. My nightie is in the way. I lift one leg, sob, and lift the other, pulling roughly at my nightie. I want my clothes off. All of a sudden I'm prickly hot. I lay on my side, gouging my neck and collarbone. No more, I cry. No more.

When the pain comes again, I'm up, pushing furiously—abdominals clenched like a large rock, warm and smooth, vagina vomiting, softest parts distended. I fight beyond the pain—the burning demands it.

Lifting my nightie, I glance through the tunnel of my legs. The floor is covered in blood; water; shit. Moaning, long and guttural like an injured child—retching furiously, nothing left to vomit. The wind howls close as if I'm caught in the roof. I call Help! but there is no one. I reach between my legs and feel the hard, hairy ball of my baby's half-born head. I whimper like a dying dog, and call again. No more, I say. Help, I splutter. No, no ... more. I cry hopelessly, resting my cheek in a pool of vomit-water.

I moan—it sounds like strangulation and longing.

With my arm stretched between my legs, I feel something soft and fluid as water—my baby's lips? Weeping more urgently, with a half-conceived desire to check for a cord around my baby's neck, I thrust my hand deeper, catching a torso as limbs land on floorboards.

I turn onto my back, holding the small, wrinkled face to mine. Her nose is congested and I put my mouth over it, suck hard and spit. I do the same to her mouth. She makes a noise, like air escaping from a balloon. She scrunches her face as if she will cry. I hear the beginning of a cry but then she sneezes, and pants. I smell damp new skin like untempered lust, almond water and virgin breath. Everything stills. The windvane stops screeching and my baby girl blinks at me, suspiciously and contentedly.

It's okay. It's okay, I say.

As the stillness settles on us, I name her ... Chelsea. I like the sound of the name. I can hear the water in it: shells and sea—shells-sea. The origin of the name is Old English. It means: river landing place, port for chalk or limestone. Not as pretty as shells and sea. I name her after the ocean.

My name means mercy and grace. Some people believe that grace is bestowed on you, like magic. I think grace is how you live your life. I believe you earn it. Grace is why you deserve mercy, and mercy is like forgiveness—it's a second chance. Sometimes the mercy is all used up on the lucky people. Sometimes there's no mercy left over for those whose grace is a bit shabby, a bit underworld.

I cradle Chelsea between my neck and shoulder, skin on skin. I lay a clean towel over her and I breathe deeply, longing for mercy.

When I arrive at the hospital, the midwife does all the usual stuff, blood pressure and temperature. She asks me how it happened. She says: Why didn't you get to the hospital in time?

I say nothing.

The midwife says that Chelsea will go into a humidicrib to warm up. She is far too cold. Why didn't you come to the hospital? What on earth happened, honey?

The 'honey' is there for good measure, but there's nothing sweet; it sounds like *Bad Mother!*

I'm hollow—I'm still at home, staring at the steaming grey placenta on stripped floorboards, wrapping my baby in towels with blood-wet hands—the wind is quiet as if I only imagined the fury, the umbilical cord limp like a spent penis.

I wanted Dean home early. Straight and sober, *please*— that's what I wanted to say. I didn't make a fuss because I had to get away from tattoo eyes, the stench of stale beer in dusty carpet, bitter man sweat. I knew my baby was coming—bodies have memories, twisted and sinewy like an umbilical cord.

The doctor comes. Her name is Dr S. Sesay. That's what her nametag says, but I know who she really is. Her name is Simbovala. I know her hands. I know her eyes like black-glass mirrors. I know the shape of her hairline, smooth around her forehead like a half-moon and then little peaks at each side like a cat's ears.

Hello, Annie, she says to the chart and then her black-glass eyes startle open, black as black, and latch onto me.

Hello, I say, crying quietly.

All will be well now, she says. She is talking about my baby girl of course, but it's her voice that gets me. You'll stay and rest a few days, she adds. Gently, using the soft of her thumb, she pulls at the skin beneath my eye and peers in.

I think you're a bit anaemic. She turns to the midwife and orders blood work.

The midwife says: So black under the eyes.

Staring into Simbovala's eyes, I feel as if I'm in a dream. I close my eyes. I'm floating in pitch-dark water, warm. For a moment, I see myself as she might see me. I feel manhandled and dirty and my eyes startle open. She smiles, takes my hands firmly in hers, doctor smooth. I am cast back. I am under the weeping willow tree of our childhood and I am in love.

Dr Simbovala Sesay turns to the midwife. Could you get hold of some toiletries?

The midwife says that she can take over from here. Simbovala Sesay gives her the black-glass look and off she goes.

I grab Simbovala's hands. Please! Don't tell my parents I'm here. You can't tell. Can you? Because of patient privacy ... Doctors can't tell.

I'll say nothing. She sighs in the heavy, humming way that I've only heard African people sigh: it is internal and it has other sounds in it, like their laughing.

I am crying, grabbing at both of her hands with both of my mine. Do you still live there?

No, she says firmly. I'll help you shower and then you must sleep.

I can manage, I say.

Nevertheless I'll help you. When she says 'nevertheless' it's like a song—there are tones in it that we don't have.

She sits me on a chair in the hospital shower. The midwife comes. Again, she offers to take over, but Dr Simbovala Sesay says crossly: Would you please attend to Mrs Morris?

Simbovala rubs soap against the washer, wiping the warm cloth across my neck and collarbone, lingering at the violet bruises—the strangling was a close call—it made me feel like someone else was there with me; like I had some control; like I could end it.

Simbovala washes my arms and hands, one bloodied fingertip at a time. Taking the showerhead, she rinses me with warm water. Smothering soap on the face washer, and more water, she spreads my knees wide, washing the blood from my inner thighs, paying attention to the flaps and folds and dried, matted blood, gently-gently, as if my intimate layers were delicate pink petals, her hands gentle as warm water, her voice smooth and bottomless as black glass.

Simbovala's voice is a quiet hum: Your mother suffered an aneurism.

I close my eyes. Time is empty; the wind stills under the willow tree. I remember that the earth never has its fill of human flesh. No matter how many people die, the earth is never satisfied. It wants more bodies. Does Simbovala Sesay remember that? Under the willow, she taught me about the insatiable earth—The earth does not get fat, she whispered in

130

my ear, again and again, her breath greedy, my neck craned, The earth does not get fat. The hair on my neck stood on end. I was panting as Simbovala summoned the dead spirits to the greedy earth, my innards buzzing and clenching without my say-so.

Dr Sesay brings me back to the present, speaking in tones like quiet men singing. Your mother died. I look down at my thighs, watch new blood pool hopelessly. It was fast. She did not suffer.

I'm cradled in warm onyx glass. Gentle hands caress my slack belly, achingly tender at my inner thighs as if I'm her broken lover—nevertheless tones humming, just for me. It's the most intimate moment I have ever known ... mercy and kindness, flailing desire, breathless wonder.

In my mind's eye I see my dad. Alone. His face repeats, camera flash on old memories. I must go to him. I have no one here. Not really.

Do you understand, Annie? Your mother is ...

The earth does not get fat. The earth does not get fat.

Chapter Eleven

The earth does not get fat

Nguni saying: 'The earth does not get fat' (i.e. however
many dead it receives the earth is never satiated)

'Proverbs in Africa', *The Wisdom of Many. Essays on the Proverb*, R. Finnegan

My best friend's name is Simbovala. I love her with all my
heart. Only I can say her name properly—Sim-bo-va-la.
Everyone else just calls her Simba. I only call her Simbovala
when we are alone. I whisper it to her when we lie down
under the weeping willow tree in my backyard. It sounds
like a secret. It makes her laugh. She laughs like the birds.
Only I can make her laugh.

Today we stare up at the sky through the branches of the
weeping willow. The branches dance like hair. Simbovala
doesn't have the dancing type of hair; hers is like sea sponge,
springy and spiky. Mostly, Simbovala wears her hair in tiny
plaits that look as though they are stuck to her head. We
break branches from the willow and wrap them around
our heads like a wreath. We pretend that we are in Africa.
Simbovala calls Africa her homeland.

When I tell Simbovala that the tree's name is weeping willow, she stops and stares at the sky. She stares up through the bendy branches and she has tears in her eyes. Now I call it the crying tree.

Simbovala teaches me how to do the cross-clapping hands that she does with her friends in the homeland. We chant *Homeland, homeland* as we walk around the trunk of the willow. Simbovala says she will walk backwards because I'm not very good at doing the cross-clapping hands and walking at the same time. We fall down in the end, sprawled and laughing. We are still there when my older brother, Cam, walks through the back gate. He says that we are queer.

That night, Cam says that I am infatuated with Simbovala. Mum says don't be so ridiculous. I look up 'infatuated' in the dictionary. It says: foolishly in love, obsessed. I am infatuated with Simbovala's laugh, I am infatuated with her hair, with the chalky-smoothness of her cross-clapping hands, with the milky half-moons on her nails.

I am the best girl speller in Grade Six. James is nearly as good as me, but he's a boy and he got 'rhythm' wrong last time. James has trouble with Simbovala's name. The first time he says it, he stumbles. I laugh, so does Simbovala. James doesn't usually stumble and he goes red. Then he calls Simbovala: The Lion Hunter. I hate James. Mum says you shouldn't hate people. I definitely hate James. I can't help it. I hate him with all my heart.

Cam says that Simbovala and I are freaks. I can't really hate Cam because he is my brother. I do hate him sometimes, but then it goes away. Cam is six years older than me. When Mum is on the phone to my aunty, she says that Cam is difficult, a trying child. Dad tells Cam to stop being an arsehole.

Simbovala tells me stories. We swap stories, like I give her Cinderella or Snow White for one about the homeland. I rush through my stories because they're just fairytales. Simbovala's stories are about real life, like her name means: While you mark out a field, Death marks you out in life. She says it reminds us that, as we live, we are in the midst of death.

I want to keep hearing it, even though it's a bit spooky, like a curse. I make her say it all the time: I pretend I can't remember; I'm infatuated with that one. She knows that I already know it, but I need to hear it out of her homeland voice.

My name is Annie. I am named after my grandmother. She is dead. Whenever I say 'dead', Simbovala says: The earth does not get fat. She says it in a voice that's like quiet men singing. It means: however many people are buried in the earth, the earth is never satisfied. Creepy hey, like the earth is after us.

I try to think up new reasons to say 'dead'. I tell her stories from the news just so that I can say 'dead', 'died', 'dying'. I tie the stringy branches of the weeping willow around my neck and I say it like Simbovala says it: The earth does not get fat, the earth does not get fat. She doesn't get creeped out. Then I say it in the voice from Cam's scary movies. That makes Simbovala laugh: she sounds like a magpie. Her laugh turns sad at the end, as if she's missing someone.

One day, Cam calls Simbovala a dark witch. I hate him so much that I think I could probably kill him. He calls her a witch because we took the radio out of his room and put it under the willow tree. I call Cam an arsehole. He is trying to hurt me because he knows that I love Simbovala with all my heart.

Simbovala says: Don't worry about Cam. She says: No polecat ever smelled its own stink. It means Cam thinks he knows everything, only he is blind because he can't see himself. She is exactly right. Cam yells at me, and at Mum and Dad, and that is the reason: he can't see that he's causing it all. That's him being difficult; that's him being trying. I'm glad he's a polecat. He hates cats.

I smile, looking up at the shapes that the bendy willow branches mark out in the sky. Simbovala says: Tell me one, so I say: Sticks and stones may break my bones but words will never hurt me.

Sometimes Simbovala gets very serious and her eyes look like black glass. She says that the songs from her homeland have matching stories and matching songs. I think of the words and the stories and the songs, all fitting together like the wooden dolls on my bookshelf, one hiding inside the other.

The proverbs are the short ones, says Simbovala, and I nod, looking straight at her eyes, just like I do to Mrs Mistle, so she knows I'm paying attention. They are for teaching a lesson, she says, like the polecat, she adds and we both laugh.

I say: Tell me another one.

The baboons laughed at one another's overhanging eyebrows, says Simbovala.

I don't get it, I say.

She says: One another's, you see, because they all have the same eyebrows, but they don't know, because baboons don't look in the mirror.

Like—you can't see past the end of your own nose.

Ooh, I like that one, she says. Imagine how big your nose would be if you couldn't see past. She laughs. Tell me another one.

That's the pot calling the kettle black, I say. I blurt it out as quickly as I can just to satisfy her, even though I know that mine are not as mysterious as hers. I tell her the first one that I can think of because she's begging me.

Sometimes I think that she only asks me to tell her some so that it's even, so that I feel like I'm giving her something back. Simbovala is quiet, like she doesn't understand, but she doesn't ask me to explain. It's because they're both black, I say. Like Cam said to Mum: You're so selfish, because she won't buy him a car, and Mum said: Now that's the pot calling the kettle black. Simbovala remains silent. It's not racist, I say, remembering that Cam is an arsehole.

I stand up and take hold of the strong, ropey branches of the willow. I pretend to swing at Simbovala. I'm a polecat, I say. I have come to return you to the earth. Simbovala laughs so hard that she has to hold her belly and curl herself into a ball on the ground. What's so funny? I ask, lying next to her so that I can feel the rumble of her laugh.

She turns over to face me. Polecats are small, she says, puffing to get her breath. They don't swing. They're like your homeland cat, but they live in the wild and they smell.

Like a skunk? I ask, thinking how generous it is that she gives me a homeland of my own, like I'm a queen or something.

A what? She says, laughing low and gurgly. She can't get a breath in. I can't answer because I'm laughing too.

At night Simbovala's stories wake me up. They are not funny. Her laugh is taken back to the earth and it echoes like voices in a cave, but the voices are dead and screaming because the earth is swallowing them, eating them alive. Baby polecat-skunks climb out of Simbovala's dead mouth and squirt their stink everywhere. I squeal and cry and Mum comes.

In the morning, Mum says that she thinks I am spending too much time with Simbovala. She says that I need to extend my friendship circle. Cam takes his earphones out of his ears. He sits opposite me at the table, chewing and listening hard. Mum doesn't even tell him to close his mouth. He crunches his cereal, eating it as revoltingly as he can, because he knows he is annoying me. He gawks at me like a stunned polecat.

I don't want to play with anyone else, I say hysterically, crying like I did in the middle of the night.

Mum says: Settle down right now, please. People are different, simple as that.

Cam says: Simbovala must have put a curse on you and that's why you're acting so fruity.

Mum says: Don't be so ridiculous and put your lunch in your bag. Then she says: What about if we invite Casey over to play on the weekend? You could sleep out in the tent under the willow tree.

Casey's a polecat, I say. Mum sips her tea. She looks into the mug, sniffs it, and then pours it down the sink. She puts her hand on my forehead, looks at her watch.

The nightmares go on and on. Always the earth is trying to eat Simbovala alive. Then the baboons chase Cam to get him to the place where the earth eats people. I hide behind the willow tree. I don't help him because I'm too scared and I don't want to die. In the dream Cam's not my brother. In the dream it doesn't matter if I don't love him.

The next afternoon we take Cam's radio again. I thought he wouldn't know; I thought he had basketball training.

Cam throws a pinecone at Simbovala. He says he was going for me because I called him a polecat. That's what he says, but he's a pretty good aim and he's a pretty good liar. The pinecone scratches Simbovala's eye, the actual eyeball, and her eye won't stop crying.

We take Simbovala home before Mum and Dad go for their walk. Dad is trying to get skinnier so Mum hides the potato chips in the laundry cupboard; she says that Dad can come with her on her walks ... even though it's her thinking time.

Simbovala's mum and dad come out onto the verandah to meet us. Her dad puts his hand out to my dad and then to Mum. His name is Mansa. He says: Call me Rex. Both names mean 'king', that's what Simbovala told me. He has a beautiful voice, a little bit scary if you were in the dark, but beautiful anyway.

Mum does the talking. She says it was an accident. She says we're very sorry indeed. She says Cam is having a troubled time at present, he thinks he knows everything, won't be told.

Aah, says Rex, showing his massive white teeth as if he is opening his mouth at the dentist. The won't-be-told man sees by the bloodstain.

Steady on, steady on, says Dad, creasing up his forehead like he's getting a headache. My stomach grumbles. Cam caused this whole thing and he's probably just relaxing, watching the telly with his feet up on the couch, eating everyone's dinner.

We're very sorry, says Mum, looking at Dad like he better *shut up* or he won't be coming on the walk.

Simbovala's brother comes out of the front door. He stands on the verandah, too, and they are all in a row.

Simbovala's brother is about the same age as Cam, but he is bigger than any man I know. His name is Neo. They didn't change his name or Simbovala's.

Mum starts up again. She is doing that thing where she is in a conversation with someone and then starts talking to herself; it's very annoying. Cam ... she starts, but then she stops and starts again. Our boy did the wrong thing. We're very sorry. If only he would listen ...

Aah, and a goat may beget an ox and a white man sew on a native head ring, says Rex, putting an arm around Neo, throwing his big head back and laughing. He sounds like Simbovala, but his laugh is deeper, more spread out. He opens his mouth really wide when he laughs and it reminds me of the baby polecats.

Just remember who you're talking to, says Dad, shifting his weight from one leg to the other. Just remember where you are, in the street with the old white man. He chuckles when he says it so it sounds friendly, only he looks a bit nervous, like when he's watching the horse races on Saturday afternoon.

It's like 'Pigs might fly', Dad, I say quietly. I look at Simbovala and she winks at me, just like Mrs Mistle when I learned to spell 'rhythm'.

Simbovala's mum's name is Amadika. She says: Call me Amy. She stretches out her hand in the direction of the front door; she stretches it slow and long like a lady dancing. She says: Will you come? Dad already took a step back when he said the thing about the white man so I know we're not going in.

Thank you, Amy, but we'll go, says Mum, pausing thoughtfully. Amy—that means 'beloved'. Mum looks pleased with herself. She looks at me as if she wants me to say: Yes, that's the way, Mum. I turn away. Amy isn't her real name and beloved is not a story.

I look at Simbovala. She has tears in her good eye. She scrunches the layers of her skirt in her hands so that the floral ruffles ride up her skinny black thigh. I can't take my eyes off her because I love her with all my heart.

Amy taps Simbovala's hand away from her skirt. Then she takes Simbovala's hand in her own. Simbovala wriggles her fingers to get free.

I want to say: Waah! I'm a polecat! I want to say it loud and close to Simbovala's face so that she will laugh. I hate Cam. I hate Dad. I especially hate Mum.

We turn around to leave. Rex keeps talking as we head out of the cracked concrete driveway. He talks in a loud voice, behind our backs, but it's not a secret from us. He's talking to all of us and to nobody at all, sort of like Mum does, except that he knows we're listening; he just doesn't need us to answer. He says: The man with the deepest eyes can't see the moon until it is fifteen days old.

Dad turns back to Mum. He says: Do you think he's having a crack at me?

Leave it alone. We're all different. We've made our peace, she says.

He's a few sheep short, I reckon, says Dad, and Mum shushes him. Can't see the wood for the trees.

The next day Simbovala does her oral presentation on 'Someone I Really Admire'. She talks about her dead grand-mother, only she doesn't say 'dead', she says 'passed over', and because she skips out on dead, she doesn't say: The earth does not get fat. She looks at me. She knows I want it.

I say it in my head because I'm addicted: The earth does not get fat, the earth does not get fat. I can't get her voice right in my mind and that scares me even more than the earth eating people.

Simbovala finishes off her presentation with a saying from her mum; she says: The dying of the heart is a thing unshared. Mrs Mistle asks her to repeat it and then she writes it up on the board. Everyone claps. James sniggers.

That saying is an arsehole, a baboon's overhanging arse-hole. I don't know why Mrs Mistle is so over the moon about it. Simbovala has never said that one before and I hate it when the parents do the homework for their kids.

It wasn't me who threw the pinecone. Sticks and stones and bones.

I didn't know you were supposed to do the talk about someone you knew. I thought it had to be, like, someone famous so I did mine about Mother Teresa. Some people say she was more like an angel than a person, but angels aren't real and she's dead now.

The earth does not get fat, the earth does not get fat.

Chapter Twelve

Sowing the wind

As you sow, so you shall reap

Proverbs and sayings

I walk down the concrete steps to the bay, carrying a basket in one hand and Chelsea on my hip. Teddy walks behind me, dragging a blow-up dinghy.

Not too close to the steps, Teddy, I say, or Shells will be up and down all day.

We move along the beach and step down over the wall of timber sleepers. Teddy takes the dinghy to the water's edge, filling a bucket with sand to weigh it down. I place Chelsea on the sand and shake out the towels. Beautiful day, I say, looking up at the sky.

When we are settled on the towels, I pass Chelsea some grapes. Teddy peels the lid from a container of dip and reaches into the basket for some biscuits.

You're a grape-guts, Miss Shells, I say, pretending to eat her chubby thigh, making chomping noises as I huddle over her, kissing her and nibbling her leg. Grape juice drizzles down her chin, and she belly-chuckles.

Sorry about last night, I say, I shouldn't have thrown the plate.

Doesn't matter.

Dad needs to ...

I hate him, he says.

Hate is exhausting, I tell him, sifting sand and shell grit between my fingers.

Does Dad know it's your birthday? Teddy helps himself to an olive, offers me one.

I shrug.

Teddy spits the olive onto the sand. That's disgusting, he says.

I LOVE those.

He rubs his nose, says: What's inside the olives?

Pimento.

Pi-what?

It's a pepper, I say, laughing.

The incoming tide laps my fingertips and the sand whips my face. I wake up, coughing sandy grit. The dinghy skips over the water like a smooth, flat stone. Chelsea's bottle and the leftover picnic lunch are strewn around the basket. I stand, suddenly and clumsily, looking back towards the road and then out to the water.

Teddy, I call, my voice croaky. Teddy? Yelling now: *Teddy?* I run along the beach to the next sleeper-wall.

Teddy! Chelsea!

I turn and sprint back along the beach, puffing and yelling. I leap up the concrete steps to the roadside, looking left and then right along the highway, yelling their names. Nothing.

Descending the steps in pairs, I bump into a woman, on the way up with her dog. I knock her hard against the bluestone wall. Spying the dinghy, further out now, I run to the water, splashing through the shallows and crying hysterically, screaming my children's names.

When I am thigh-deep in water, I look back to the shore. The woman is brushing sand from her pants in abrupt, smacking strokes, muttering to her dog on a leash, watching me.

I plunge in. The water is freezing. The dinghy is now only a flash of yellow, hopscotching over the white-capped waves. I swim in the direction of the dinghy, but I can barely see it anymore. It skitters over the water like a small yellow bird, airborne one moment, duck-diving the next.

I realise that my children couldn't be in the dinghy if it is flying around like that. I swim back towards the shore, back to where I can wade and then run. Their names are distorted by my wailing. My words are barely recognisable. The breath has been sucked out of me. I am winded.

The woman approaches the water's edge as I get close to shore. I charge past her to the picnic, holding the stitch in my side.

She says: What's wrong?

I vomit violently, gasping for breath between explosions. The black labrador sniffs and licks at the vomit. Get out of it, Pony, says the woman. She turns to me: What's wrong?

My children, I say, straightening up, wiping my nose and gasping for air. I can't find them.

Sow the wind; reap the storm, she says.

What did you say?

Oh nothing. I'm not sure why that came to me just now. I'll call the police, shall I?

I sit in the interview room, looking around, taking the place in, reading the Police Code of Ethics—strive to serve with integrity and ...

The policeman comes very close. He says that my story does not add up, but not all stories do, even when they're true. The policewoman is following his lead.

She says: May I call you Annie?

Okay, I say. I'm thinking she can call me whatever she wants, as long as she finds the children. Her nametag says Constable Janice Coles. She is by the book, green as.

Annie, we'll tape this interview today, says Coles.

I should be at the beach, I say, moving my hands from the table to my lap, and then back again. How long will this take?

Well that depends, says Mills.

I stand up, clenching my fists over the back of the chair.

We'll be as brief as possible, says Mills. *Sit down, please.*

He is treating me like a criminal. He thinks I've been sowing the wind for years.

Tell me about the last time you saw your children, says Mills, sipping his cup of coffee noisily.

I say: We had a picnic. Chelsea went to sleep. Did they get her little lamb from the beach?

What happened after the young one went to sleep?

She needs her lamby, I say. I have a spare one at the house.

Mills shifts his chair, scraping it noisily along the floorboards and bringing himself as close to the table as possible.

Teddy and I caught crabs near the sleeper-wall, I say. He doesn't like to keep them out of the water long, so ...

145

The sleeping-wall?

Sleeper, I say. Wood, I add, recalling the weather-beaten post against my back, the splintery brightness of the stars ...

Groyne, says Mills, correcting me. They are called groynes.

I pay no attention to him because I'm thinking about that first night with Dean. I'm wondering why, even then, I knew to hold on to the post, rather than to him. Groyne sounds like a made-up word anyway. Mills just wants to prove he's smarter than Coles and quite frankly I think they're both a bit behind the eight ball.

Mills gets in my face, he says: What time did the child go to sleep? He speaks slowly, calculating the impact of each word.

What? Oh, it must have been two, nearly two. She ...

Coles narrows her eyes at me, brushing her silky hair away from her face: Does the baby often sleep at the beach?

I put my hand to my own hair, thick with sandy grit, waxy from the salt wind. I fix on Coles for just a moment and then I shift my gaze to the window, to the wind in the trees. In summer Chelsea sleeps under the umbrella so that Teddy can swim.

Coles refers to her notes. Teddy was not at school.

I already told you that.

Yes. Was he unwell?

No.

Why was Teddy home from school?

I said he could have the day off because he didn't sleep very well. We had a fight ...

What did you fight with Teddy about?

Not Teddy. Dean. My ...

Your husband?

146

We're not married, I say.

Coles says: What did you and Dean fight about?

Nothing. He's paranoid, I say.

Coles looks over at Mills.

Coles says: What is he paranoid about? Remember that anything you tell us will help us find the children.

Dean always worries that I've been with someone else or that I will be with someone else. He's very possessive.

I stop there and turn to the window. The view has altered. I can only see the tops of the trees, but it's clear that the wind has switched, changed direction, like the truth. Everything looks different.

Coles shifts her chair closer to the table. She says: Is Dean the children's father?

Y-yes, I say.

You don't sound so sure, she adds, leaning across the table.

I say: Sorry, is this a paternity hearing? Fuck her.

Coles looks at Mills.

We're trying to find the children, says Mills. Is Dean the children's father?

Yes, I say. Fuck him, too.

I walk over to the window. Within the hour, Port Phillip Bay has become an ocean beach. Where would the dinghy be now? Point Lonsdale? Queenscliff? Tasmania?

A whole hour, *Gone.* I don't know where the children are. I need to know where they are. I don't give a fuck what the police think about me. I just want my children.

The interview room is on the first floor of the building, two hundred metres from the beach. I can see right out to the horizon and then, below me, I can see into a hundred backyards. The wind belts the towels on a nearby clothesline, whipping them up and over, twisting them in knots. Beach wind is different. It's not just the smell of the sea.

Mills speaks loudly: What did you do when the child went to sleep? He stands in front of me, blocking the view from the window.

I stand tall, trying to see over his shoulder.

He says it again, loud and angry: What did you do when the child went to sleep?

Red sky at night, sailor's delight, I say. It's all I can think of.

Mills says: What do you mean? This is no time for …

Coles says: Focus. *Please!* Time is of the essence here.

Time? I say, turning to her for a moment and then back to Mills. I move to the left so I can see out. Red sky in the morning, sailor's warning, I say sleepily, resuming my vigil at the window.

What are you talking about?

It's supposed to be about the colour of the sky, I say, but it's always about the wind.

Mills recaps loudly, his breath bitter: Chelsea was asleep. *Where were you?* He stands steadfast, wiping the foamy saliva from the corners of his mouth. *What did you do?*

Teddy took the boat out. He was walking around there … I point out to the water, bumping my knuckles against the windowsill. I shake my head: In the shallows, near the yacht.

Did you see anyone, talk to anyone?

A man walked past.

What time was that?

But he seemed normal.

Mills scratches behind his ear. Can you tell us anything defining about the man: hair, clothes, age?

Coles speaks before I can get a word in: What did you have for the picnic?

What? Mills speaks sharply, glaring at Coles.

I laugh. They both stare at me because I'm laughing, because I'm behaving like the wind. I don't care what they think. I only care about my children. They tricked me into coming and now they won't let me go; they think I'm culp-able. I want to be out there looking for my children. I can't concentrate on anything they say. My mind is at the beach.

Mills says: How old was the man?

I eyeball him. His eyes are slightly different colours, or maybe it's the glint from the window that makes the left one look more grey than blue. His hair is silver-grey and it makes his eye ...

How old?

He had a limp, I say. God, what's the time now? I take a step closer to the window, my face almost against it, rubbing my hand up and down the aluminium window frame.

The window doesn't open, says Coles, removing my hand from the frame. The muscles in her forearms are taut and defined. Her skin is silky smooth and pale. I stare at her hands and forearms and she shifts them to her side, letting them hang beside her slender legs, alongside her flat stomach. She is not thin: she is exercise-junky skinny.

Did anyone else pass you on the beach today? Mills speaks slowly and clearly.

No, I say.

Was ...

Hang on, I say. There was a group of women, a walking group. The leader had a rod, a stick. I hold my arm out to the side, imitating. She was calling out instructions.

Never mind about that, says Mills.

Coles steps forward, chest out. When you last saw the children, they were in the boat.

No.

Your friend said that you were chasing the boat—the woman with the labrador. Coles takes a few steps back, refers to her notes on the table. Janelle, she says.

I don't know her, I say, my voice high. What else did *she* say?

Mills takes a deep breath and then speaks loudly: Where did you last see the children *before* they were missing?

Teddy was in the water. Chelsea was asleep.

Mills turns to Coles and sighs loudly, cracks his knuckles. I can't make heads or tails of this, he mumbles. He puts his hands behind his head and stretches his elbows back. Look here, Annie, he says in his bastard voice. Any hope of finding the children depends ...

I fell asleep! I yell.

And when you woke up they were gone, says Coles.

Yes. *Fuck.* I was exhausted. I didn't mean it.

Mills fiddles with his bushy eyebrows, grunts loudly. Coles makes her way back to the table and takes up her pen. She stands over the notepad, writes something down and underlines it twice. Then she puts the pen down and approaches me. Do you think it's possible that Teddy took the baby?

Where? Where would he go? Teddy wouldn't take Chelsea. The beach is his favourite place.

If he was upset and confused about the fight ...

He wasn't upset, I say, staring her down.

Teddy's behaviour could be very out of character. In these situations ...

Situations! This is not a fucking …

Settle down please, missy, says Mills. If we could get a better idea of time, of about how long they'd been missing when you woke up.

I can't believe he called me Missy. I want to shove a groyne post up his arse.

Before you go, just read this please, and sign here. It indicates that we have undertaken an interview today. It will stay on our system, that's a protocol thing. It's a reference for us … nothing on you. Coles clears her throat, clarifies, nothing listed against you, that is, only it'll stay open to view. I need your date of birth in there, too, for our records, and then Sergeant Mills will take you to …

Coles reaches her hand out towards me. Oh dear … It's your … Happy, um, birthday.

Grace leads me through a series of doors and into a room: white walls, white linoleum floors. Teddy is lying on a stainless-steel trolley. The trolley is covered with a white sheet. Teddy's body is covered by another sheet. Grace leads me to him.

Teddy has a mole above his knee, on his right thigh, exactly the same spot as mine.

Grace removes the sheet covering Teddy's body. She lifts the medical gown so that I can see the mole.

I'm sorry, I cry. I'm so sorry. I brush Teddy's hair back and kiss his forehead. He looks asleep but smaller than he was before. Oh God, he's so small, littler than today.

Oh, fucking God; I hate Dean; I fucking hate him. I turn to Grace: Can I hold him?

Of course. You'll need to sit down, honey. He'll feel heavy to you because he can't hold himself anymore. I'll help you with him.

Grace brings a chair and I sit. She walks over to the bench along the far wall. She brings back a packet of jellybeans and, discreetly, shows them to me. She says: Can I give these to Chelsea?

I nod.

Grace opens the jellybeans and holds them out to Chelsea. Look what I have for you, Chelsea. Look. When Chelsea has one jellybean in her mouth, and one in each of her hands, Grace pours the rest of the packet into an empty coffee mug, places a teaspoon in the mug and stirs them around. Grace crouches on the floor, just beside my chair, rattling the lollies in the mug. These are for you, sweetie-pie, says Grace, placing the mug on the floor. Chelsea wriggles down from my lap.

Grace is level with me now. She holds one of my hands and strokes my forearm. She speaks quietly in rhythm with her movements. It'll look a bit awkward when I pick him up, but I'll be as gentle with him as I possibly can, she says. He'll feel cold to you, and heavy. He can't support his head or his arms or legs. Okay, honey, are you ready?

I stretch out my arms to show that I am ready. Everything seems to be happening in slow motion. There is only the rattling of the jellybeans and my moaning. With her back to me, Grace scoops Teddy up from the trolley. He looks stiff, like driftwood. She places Teddy in my lap and I kiss his forehead, eyelids, lips—I'm going to vomit, I say.

Grace grabs a silver dish from the bench and rushes to me. Shall I take him?

No, I say. Don't take him. I am trying to vomit and I am trying to get the words out. Please don't take him.

Grace holds the dish up to my mouth and I heave but there is only foamy saliva. Do I have to go? I say.

You *do not* leave here until you're ready, she says. When did you last eat or drink anything?

We had a picnic ...

Teddy's head lolls awkwardly in the crook of my arm, his mouth is open and awful. Grace squats beside me and holds Teddy's head.

Chelsea is grinning, jellybean juice dribbling down her chin. T-ed, she says, her bright toddler cheeks up against his drowned-dead face.

I am heaving and moaning. It is a type of crying. It's like the birth noise.

Yes, Chelsea, it's Teddy, says Grace.

I dry-retch again. I feel empty except that I love them both, so fucking much. My love for Teddy is still here— it's like a punch in the stomach: it winds me and makes me vomit.

She-can't-understand. She-won't-understand. Where-he-is. Where-he's-gone.

No, she won't, says Grace. It's too hard to understand.

The beach is his favourite place. He would have been frightened and it's his best place.

I know, honey.

I stroke Teddy's forehead. He loves it when I do this, I say. I heave, choke, swallow and gag.

He called out to me. I think that's when I woke up. The children weren't there anymore; they were both gone. I was sure I heard Teddy calling me and I didn't know if it was true or a dream, but I definitely heard it. I can still hear it. The calling and the wash of the waves; it's all I hear.

The love is the same, I say. I want to tell her that there's all this filthy yearning too, because the love has nowhere to settle. It is sucked in and out relentlessly, like vomiting waves. It's so thick and I can't breathe and he's calling me, he needs me.

I love the wind, I say because I still want to love it.

Chapter Thirteen

Clay

Clays are plastic due to their water content and become hard, brittle and non-plastic upon drying ... Depending on the content of the soil, clay can appear in various colours, from white to dull [grey] or brown to a deep orange-red.

https://en.wikipedia.org/wiki/Clay

Yesterday I dug a hole for him, yesterday and most of the night. My palms are blistered. I am grateful for the rawness, burning and throbbing like cracked nipples, keeping sleep at bay, out in the bay. I am frightened to fall asleep because I may dream him, crying and gurgling and calling for me, out in the cold, dark wash.

I dug a hole for him near the laundry because it's his favourite place, close to the house, close to the beach ... The afternoon sun catches there, lingering, browning his knobbly knees. The lawn is thick and green and the gusty breeze sweeps his sandy fringe off his face as he plays. His hands are always busy, building something with shells and twigs, stones and pinecones. He blinks and laughs, throwing his head back. He loves to play there. *Sorry.* He *loved* to play there. Past tense. How can this be?

I worried that the hole wasn't deep enough, so I set to digging again, blisters bleeding. I dug until the loose earth was level with my breasts, thinking I would lay him in the earth, just as he is, wrapped in a large tartan blanket. But the earth has turned to clay—ugly, thick, windless. Teddy loves the wind and I can't put him against clay. Clay does not care for wind. Clay does not care for anything.

What can I put him in? What will I do?

Love means you will do anything. Love means you will do all the things you thought you would never do—cock against your gullet—even if it makes you sicker than vomit and lonely as death, you will do it. That's what love actually means.

I sit on the back step in the charcoal evening light, waiting for Pelts to bring Teddy from the morgue. He parks the car at the side of the house and carries Teddy in, zipped in a bag. Pelts turns sideways to get Teddy in the door. He glances towards the hole, the ugly mound of clay, sticky thick and hopeless under the fluorescent light.

I lead Pelts to Teddy's bed and roll back the covers. He lays Teddy there, gently, and looks at me. Go, I say quietly. Come back just before daylight.

Pelts speaks slowly. Shall I take—

I interrupt. She is already asleep, I say emptily.

I unzip Teddy's head. It's not enough and it was never going to be enough so I unzip everything.

I fill a tub with water, so warm, and I carry the water to Teddy. I wash every bit of him: every dip, every nook. I kneel beside him, on the zip bag, and the zip digs into my knees like what might have been.

156

I dress him in his striped blue pyjamas and I wipe his face, again and again, rubbing extra soap around his neck and face until he smells familiar. His face feels like clay. I try to see beyond what I feel with my own warm hands. I say: I love you, Teddy. I love you very, very much.

Then I do his voice. I say: I love you, too, Mum. I love you with all my heart. It sounds wrong. I cry desperately.

I walk from room to room, trying to find something to hold him before he goes in the hole. I say, *fucken, fucken, fucken shitty life* and then I say, *get it together right now*. I pour a glass of water and put the kettle on, thinking I'm probably a bit dehydrated from all the digging—nothing to eat, nothing much to drink.

I take the milk out of the fridge to make a cup of tea. The milk is not cold and it smells wrong so I tip it down the sink, lurching after it. There is nothing, only lurching and a clay-cold face. I check the thermostat inside the fridge. Although it is up to the max, the fridge is barely cold. I know immediately that this is where I will put him. Perhaps I knew before now, because the hole seems to have been dug with the fridge in mind. I begin to take the things out: butter, a bruised apple, wilted carrots.

I take the scissors and go back to Teddy, cutting some of his golden hair. I carry it to the kitchen, emptying the tea bags from the box so I can put the hair in there—it looks accidental, like a mistake. I wasn't careful enough about making sure that the box was empty of tea dust and it is a stupid idea anyway, because his hair doesn't smell the same in the box. Nothing smells the same. Nothing is the same.

Smells and images collide. My mind is cluttered like an op-shop. Earl grey tea, citrus bergamot—Teddy's ashen cheeks. Palmolive soap, wafting freesia—Teddy's sunken eyes. Sour milk, glugging in the plughole—Teddy's bittersweet neck. Tea and soap, milk and skin, simple things have become twisted. The smells are sticking to me; there's no everyday air.

Teddy's eyes look bruised. His lips are purple and closed as if they never opened. He is no longer a soft boy but a painted, rigid doll. I return to the kitchen, filling the sink with hot water, disinfectant and soap. I take the grater and I grate Teddy's soap into the hot, hot water. Then I take out the wire racks and I scrub the inside surfaces of the fridge, bending into the depthless white so that I can smell as I go, so that I can be sure that it smells like him.

I remove the screws that hold the freezer compartment in place, wrenching it out. I cut the electrical cord with the big kitchen knife, denting the floorboards because the cord is so stubborn. I take some steel wool and scour desperately at the tracks that held the wire shelves in place—wire smells like blood, like a cage or a garden rake, not like him. The steel wool shaves my blisters like razor blades, like regret. I clean the outside of the fridge as furiously as I have cleaned the inside. I know the fridge will get dirty as soon as it hits the earth, but it will be clean first—I will make sure of it.

I rub Teddy's doona and pillow with a dry cake of soap. I lay the doona on the inside of the fridge to soften it, trying to make it look less like a fridge and more like a bed. I keep the pillowcase because it smells like Teddy's breath. It smells like my darling boy, laughing in the wind. I loop it through my frayed bra strap, bending my head towards it as I work, greedy for his smell.

Then I go and get him, lifting him gently as if he's fallen asleep in the car, as if I'm carrying him inside to bed. As I lay him in the fridge he looks beautiful, superb, too good to be true. If he were any taller he wouldn't fit in the fridge—he is stuck straight like a cricket bat. My beautiful, soft boy—a cricket bat in a broken fridge, dead wood in a fridge coffin.

What am I thinking? Is this real? Am I awake?

I tuck more blankets around him, tight around him, so he can't come undone, so that he can't wriggle around when I put him in the ground. I can't cover his face, not yet, not ever in fact so I put more blankets around him and around him. He looks like a newborn baby, his dear little face poking out of the blankets. It makes time seem like a dream, it makes all of my time with him seem like a wish, something that I wanted too much, so much that I imagined it hard and it seemed real, only it could never be as real as I wanted it to be because he was too good to be true.

I take the large tartan blanket into the kitchen, lifting one corner of the fridge and then the other, wriggling the blanket under the weight of it, inch by inch. I am sweating, crying and moaning, thinking that I will never be able to get the blanket under the fucking weight of that fucking fridge. I consider giving up, taking him out and putting him in the hole just as he is, but then I remember the clay, thick and suffocating as a dead boy's skin.

Lifting the fridge door, I breathe his dear little face, knowing that I will do what I set out to do, for him I can do anything because I love him—fucking-fucking-love—and even if he becomes thick without his smell, and rank, even if I cannot stop it, my hands will not move him closer to the clay.

Once the blanket is under the fridge, I push him and drag him towards the laundry. I stop a minute, my head in my palms, sobbing deep, breathless breaths, and for a time there is calmness, some sort of reprieve, a wafting. I know that it is not quite sleep. I can feel his warmth against my chest, panting his precious breath against my neck.

Opening the fridge, I kiss his clay lips. I hold my lips against his and I know that he is too dead to be true. I will get him out to the earth. I will get him near the water where there is wind. Because he loves me, I can do anything.

I open the laundry door so that only the flywire separates me from the backyard grave. I open the fridge and kiss the rubber meat of his lips, stiff and sour raw, room temperature and wrong. I kiss him until the air is thick, like clay against my windpipe. Leaning left of the fridge, I vomit, but nothing comes. I heave and heave and it sounds like an echo because it goes on and on, like ugly, directionless love, like squally wind.

I lay beside the fridge, on the edge of the tattered tartan blanket. I gasp, on the cusp of sleep. I lift the door and kiss him one last time, holding my lips there without breathing, until I know, with raging disgust, that my lips will never touch his again. I can't bear the thought that the fridge will open on the way down so I bind it tight with string, two balls of twine sawing at my open blisters. The blisters weep and bleed like stigmata. I hope they never heal.

Pelts arrives and I realise I have forgotten time. Dawn is an hour away. The light shifts to jaundiced grey as we drag the fridge towards the clay mound. We stand beside the hole, pulling first and then pushing, heaving. Teddy thumps in head first, on a bit of an angle. It is fast in the end and I land on top of him. My weight against the fridge pushes his bottom half down. I lay there in a trance, eyes wide.

Pelts pulls me out of the hole. I am very dizzy so I lay on the ground, my cheek against the clay. I wonder what happened during the night when time stopped. I want to open the fridge door and see him one last time. I can't believe that he is in there even though I have seen it with my own eyes. I lay on the earth above him, considering how I will prise the fridge door open, then I worry that I will let some clay in and I *stop*, knowing that I must leave him alone in the timeless place.

Putting the earth over him does not feel right. The rest of it I wanted to do, only I could have done it, but putting the earth over him feels wrong, like a sin. I don't believe in sins. I believe in coffins and funerals for the sons of lucky mothers, the beautiful people with money and choices and time for mourning.

I could almost leave Teddy uncovered, except that someone might find him and tamper with him, and that would be worse than covering him with earth.

I pick up a spade. I can cover him with earth because I know that no one can touch him, now or ever again. I know that every last touch on him was from me and I know what those touches were like. Only my mother-hands can touch his rubber-clay body with fire-love.

He is covered with earth and I am racked with chainsaw sobbing. Falling to the ground, I lay my cheek against clay. Pelts carries me inside and lays me in Teddy's bed. He brings the big doona from my room and tucks me in tight like a dead boy. Perhaps I sleep, although I am awake, all the while, because I will never sleep in the old way again. Sleep is gone like earl grey tea. I hear Pelts getting Chelsea up and giving her breakfast. I hear it as if I am dreaming someone else's life and I wonder whether my mother-love will survive. In the face of dead love, I wonder if it's possible. Where will the Teddy love go? His love for me is still here. It feels like clay, suffocating thickness setting in my stomach.

I sing the bath song from when Teddy was a baby. He would fall asleep in my arms, in the warm bathwater. He would cry when I lifted him out because he was cold. I would sing to him so that he knew I was there, so that he knew he would be warm soon. Even as a little boy he would have me sing the bath song as he pulled on his pyjamas. I'd hum it to him when he was sick, patting his forehead, sweeping his fringe away like the gentle wind. He never grew tired of it.

The song has nothing to do with the bath. It is about mother-love. I try to sing it now, but it sounds cracked and awful, so I hum it in my mind and whimper like a kicked dog. I close my eyes for a good while and I am on him, on the earth. After a time, I open my eyes and I wonder where I was when my eyes were closed, because I was not awake or asleep. Then I don't care where I was because I was with him.

Eventually, I move into some sort of sleep. I dream of the hole filled with seawater, of clay mixed with rich, dark soil, all of it roiled together in the sea-grave pit—a clay-cold face simmers out of the earth. All the ugliness comes together in the mottled light outside the laundry door, a fluorescent pantomime—spotlight on poor people's manky choices.

In my hand I have a handful of Teddy's pillowcase—blistery hands caked in clay-blood and weeping ooze. Clutching his pillowcase, I sleep, clenching cloth and clay, dreaming restlessly. I wake suddenly, gasping desperately, because I have lost the smell of him.

Chelsea stands beside my bed holding her lamby, sucking her thumb. She takes her thumb out momentarily. *Mum?* she says, like it's a question.

Hello, my precious angel, I whimper. I inhale sharply. Whimper again. Come, I say. I pull back the doona and she crawls into Teddy's bed, huddling in the curve of my belly where it is warm, sucking her thumb. I hum the bath song. It's all I've got. It's jagged, but the tune is recognisable, nevertheless.

Chapter Fourteen

A wake

Definitions of Wake and Their Implications
[T]he wake is 'a vigil celebrated with junketing and dancing'.
The word primarily means, of course, to prevent someone
from sleeping, to wake the person up, to disturb the person's
slumber and make it impossible for him or her to slip back
into it. The 'junketing and dancing' take place in order
to wake the person up again. That is why, compared with
ordinary social [behaviour], wakes stand out as wild and
unrestrained: They have to be 'fit to wake the dead'.

Encyclopedia of Death and Dying 2012

It's my turn to talk. I have listened to Mum and Pelts fiercely,
at our evening gatherings in front of the fire. Now it's my
turn. My question has been the same since the beginning. I
ask it, loud and clear: Where is Teddy buried?

After a short silence, Mum says: I will show you. She
stands, walking towards the laundry, slowly, like an old lady.
Turning back, she takes my hand. She opens the laundry
door, standing as still as stone on the concrete step.

Here? I say desperately. Is he here? It's no more than a
strangled whisper.

Mum takes a deep breath and steps out ten regular paces,
counting them aloud as she heads towards the enormous old

pine tree. When she gets to ten she slips off her shoe, leaving it on the grass to mark the spot. Then she walks over to the trunk of the enormous pine, stepping the paces out again from that side, heading back towards us, counting aloud. She arrives at the same spot, slipping her foot back into the shoe. Here, she says. Teddy is buried here.

She crouches down and takes some grass and topsoil in her hand. Muttering, she rubs the grass and earth between her palms. I can't make out the words. There is a rhythm—like a spell, only musical. She's singing. It's the bath song ...

I want to dig down, I say. I need to know that he is definitely there. My voice quivers but it's strong. Tomorrow we dig, I say firmly.

Pelts heads out early for boutique beer. He buys champagne, white wine, and an exorbitant bottle of red. He decants the red, placing the glass jug on the lounge-room table. He fills the laundry tub with ice and booze.

Pelts gets busy preparing a range of food. He asks me to sample things as he goes, as if we're preparing for a party, as if we're expecting guests—salmon and dill focaccia, miniature toasts with caramelised onion and marinated fetta, a platter with olives and cheese, dips, marinated mushrooms.

In the crisp late morning, I lead Mum to a deck chair and get the bocce set out for Grandad. He can play for hours, no rules—the rhythmic thwack of coloured ball against coloured ball—he laughs delightedly on impact: an old man's laugh ghosted by boyish delight.

It's all quite civilised except that we're about to unearth a grave. As Pelts and I walk to the designated burial site, a fast-moving, low-lying cloud passes overhead—the morning flickers grey and shadowy as if a light has short-circuited. The cloud passes momentarily and the sun is out again by the time our spades slice the earth.

We dig awhile, furiously. I stop to catch my breath and look over at Mum. I say: Mum? Are you sure it's okay with you? The digging. *Mum?*

Yes, Shells.

If she'd said no I'm not sure what I'd have done. I am determined to dig. I need proof. Mum, you look pale. How do you feel?

She rubs her palms up and down her face. She says: Awake, Shells, I feel awake.

Well it is a 'wake', says Pelts. I'm not being facetious. I don't mean to be … but it is Teddy's wake, isn't it? I mean it probably is …

We all glance at each other nervously and then I explode with laughter. I move to a different level of laughing. I'm laughing so hard that I'm crying. I wipe away the tears with my clay hands, painting streaky clay stripes across my cheeks.

Pelts brings a tub with hot water, a face washer and soap, so we can wash our hands after we dig, so we have clean hands to eat. He stares at me as he washes his hands and then he is still, holding his hands together as if he were praying, fingers wrapped tightly around knuckles.

He takes a piece of soft clay and dunks it in the water tub, painting his cheeks like mine. I take the clay from Pelts and wander over to Mum, wiping the clay across her cheeks. Grandad won't be left out of the fun so we take care of him, too. He wants it everywhere, a full mask. We look like we're preparing for some kind of tribal ritual. We look ridiculous. As the clay dries, it stiffens our skin like plaster. Every smile feels like more than it is, every frown, so intentional.

Music? says Pelts and I nod. He sets the stereo on the washing machine and puts the speakers through the laundry window. He chooses Celtic jigs and reels and pumps it up. It's a good choice, fast and dizzy, no words. We don't need too many words today.

At some point, Pelts refills the sink with beer and ice because it feels like thirty-three degrees, rather than twenty-three, digging in the sun. Nobody is interested in water or anything soft—soft drinks are unsuitable for waking the dead. We knock back cold stubbies to quench our thirst: fast, seamless sips to wash away the morbidity. We sip the beer, drinking fast and digging fast, in time with the music.

I mix a shandy for Grandad and resume the digging work. The music matches our momentum. I take on the rhythm of the reel, pounding the spade into the earth. My fingers dance against the green glass of the stubby as I take a long sip. Mum is jigging her knees slowly, up and down.

I stop suddenly, breathing heavily. Go easy, I say, taking hold of Pelts's arm. We don't want to … break him up.

He's in a fridge, remember? says Mum.

Would it still be intact? I rest my weight on the spade, puffing steadily. Sweat dribbles from my forehead down my clay cheeks, like muddy tears. I pause, drawing breath after breath. There is nothing more to say about the fridge. We all stop because it's a dead moment.

I can't believe you dug this all alone, I say finally. I speak loudly, so that my voice will carry over the music, so that Mum can hear me loud and clear over the steadily growing mound of clay. I say: I can't believe there's so much clay. It looks like more it was before, now that we've interfered with it. How did you do it, Mum? How did …

There was nothing else I could do, she says, shrugging. Her voice breaks on 'else' and the air becomes thick.

Shall I fire up the barbecue? says Pelts.

I wonder if it's okay to cook a barbecue when you're digging up a grave. It seems cannibalistic or something.

Pelts says: I have Greek lamb, butterfly lamb, and marinated chicken strips. We should eat or we'll be as pissed as maggots in no time.

Yes please, I say. Fire up the barbecue.

Pelts brings everything to the table: Greek salad and bread, roasted potato and sweet potato. We polish off our stubbies. He pours champagne and white wine, too many glasses for the three of us, and lemonade for Grandad. I turn the music down a little, just while we eat.

I have special red wine for tonight, Annie-girl, says Pelts. You'll love it.

It's after three before we are seated at the table. My shoes are slick, thick with clay. I'm dirty and exhausted from the digging. I look around the table and I feel lucky, proud of my ramshackle family. Pelts has the shock of wind in his hair and the hazy glaze of hard work in his eyes. Mum looks pale and sleepy but serene. There's a touch of pink to her cheeks. Grandad is tucking into the lamb, his lips glossy with the juices, his eyes sparkling with the pleasure of it.

Bon appétit, says Pelts, holding up his glass.

We clink our glasses together.

I say: If the ground was up to Mum's shoulders when she was standing in the hole—I mean, if the grave was as deep as she is tall, and there's a fridge in there, too, then we must be getting close. Unless we have the wrong spot.

Pelts chews and swallows, pauses in the slick, thick reality that we are unearthing a grave, digging the pent up, waking dead things.

You're very close, says Mum. There's no mistake about the place.

Pelts serves everyone more lamb. He talks about the old days when Teddy and I were children, playing under the ancient pine tree. He says: I remember Teddy playing out here—

Grandad interrupts: Me?

No, Grand, I say. Remember I had a brother. He had the same name as you; he was named after you. He died. He's buried in that hole. I'm making sure he's still there.

Oh, says Grandad. Where else could he be?

Nowhere, I say.

We get stuck into the digging again after lunch. I turn the music back on, the same CD, more reels and jigs, because the Irish know what they're on about; they know that happy and sad are not so different; they know that when things get tough, you need to party harder than ever. The music is not really civilised for gravedigging, and it's highly appropriate too: the tempo, the wordless, fire-cracking, love-sweaty energy.

We've had a skinful of wine and beer; we keep on anyway, drinking and digging. By the time Pelts's spade hits the fridge, metal on metal, an empty twang, there's not much sun left on the west side of the house—the wind has picked up and swung around. My spade clangs against the fridge a split second later, like a cymbal. I grab hold of Pelts's arm and that's the end of the digging.

I start weeping. I always thought crying and weeping were the same—they're not. There's the mourning noise when we weep, like a donkey braying. I get down on my hands and knees in the hole and scoop the clay from the fridge by hand. Pelts follows my lead. It is warmer in the hole, because we're protected from the wind, but Mum and Grandad are feeling the cold. Pelts heads inside to get jumpers and coats.

The daylight is getting dingy now and it makes our clay faces look whiter. The spotlight from the laundry lights our faces. Our plaster masks glow like we're in a play.

Mum heads over to the edge of the hole and Pelts lowers her in. I'll light us a fire, he says, heading to the shed. He returns, dragging a fire drum towards the hole, placing it near Mum's chair. The drum is made from the old electric hot-water system. It used to be in the roof. It looks like an enormous tin can. Pelts explains that when he renovated the bathroom, he put in a new gas system and he took the old drum out of the roof, splitting it lengthways and welding the rounded outer sides together. It makes a perfect, portable fire drum.

He fills the drum with paper and pinecones and loads of kindling. When he has it firing, he adds the ti-tree logs, the smaller pieces first. It smells like beach incense. The earthy smoke of ti-tree timber mixes with the perfume of the pinecones and the salty breath of the sea. He throws in the bushy branches, covered in ti-tree leaves. When the spray of leaves hits the flames they spark, like tiny white lights, like fireflies.

Pelts heads inside to get the decanted bottle of red. He passes us a glass, down in the hole, explaining that it was bottled the same year that Teddy was born.

I'm busy shifting the clay off the fridge door. I do it tenderly, kneeling down. I have the soap and water down there, and I'm cleaning the rusty old fridge door as if it were a tombstone, as if I'm trying to decipher the inscription, making sure I'm on the right grave. I pause and stand, taking a long sip of the velvety red wine. I drink slowly, steadily, breathing deeply through my nose until the glass is drained.

I return to the work and, after a time, the old fridge is as clean as a whistle in its bed of clay. It looks like a coffin except that it is wider. The reality of the gravedigging is urgent now that we can see the fridge. Everyone is quiet. We will soon run out of daylight so Pelts gets the portable spotlight, and we shine it towards the hole. He plants a big battery lantern in the middle of the table, amongst the remnants of lunch. He pours more wine and throws extra logs on the fire. Lastly, he gets some mozzie coils and candles in glass holders, placing them around the hole.

Grandad has been playing bocce all day, talking to himself, laughing wildly. Time for some warm clothes, old mate, says Pelts. Then you can have some cake. Your favourite— chocolate. Pelts steadies Grandad as he steps into a pair of long pants, settling him in front of the fire with a piece of cake in each hand. Grandad watches the flames like television, mesmerised by the orange-and-white dance of firelight.

I say: I have to know he's in there. I know it's morbid and weird, but all of this is whack and I need to know for sure. Get Mum *out,* I say.

Pelts pulls her up.

Mum sits near the fire and Pelts brings a blanket for her legs and a scarf for her neck. Then he heads to the shed to get a crowbar. For a split second, I feel guilty, like we're doing something very wrong.

Pelts drops himself in beside me and I hitch a lift out because there's only room for one person if the fridge door is to be opened. I crouch next to the hole on my hands and knees, torso long, arms outstretched. I don't know why I'm reaching out like that, it doesn't make sense—I do it instinctively. I shiver. I'm not cold. I feel like a criminal.

Pelts heaves the crowbar back and forth. He is groaning and it goes on a long time. Grandad gets a bit distracted by the noise and I grab him another piece of cake and throw some ti-tree branches on the fire.

Pelts stops with the crowbar so I presume he's in. He keeps the fridge door ajar, holding the crowbar steady, handing the top end of it to me. I hold on tight as he heaves himself out of the hole. Standing beside me, Pelts takes hold of the crowbar with one hand, helping me into the hole with the other. He reaches towards his feet and passes me one of the candles.

I'm in and out quickly. It's so fast after all that digging. I see a skull. I see ribs. I see a long leg bone. Skull, ribs, femur—candlelit bones in a fridge coffin. It looks like the bones are swimming, as if Teddy is still in the sea. I don't know if it's the candlelight making the bones glisten or if it's wet in there. I don't want to know. Blatant bones in a briny rust bucket, proof enough of an alive-dead brother.

Pelts helps me out of the hole. He says: Shall I shut it now, Shells?

I nod. Mum nods too—well sort of, her head drops to her chest.

We sit around the fire, keeping vigil. We're only a step or two from the hole. Pelts fills everyone's drinks.

I stand and move close to the hole, the warmth of the fire against my back. The others follow suit—without a word.

It's like a corroboree. I don't know anything about corroborees except I saw a show on the ABC: the fire and the music and the feeling that something momentous is going on between the living and the dead.

I can hear the waves, far off, and the music, close up. We stand around the hole. We don't move. No one is talking and time stands still—only the waves and the music to mark the undertow of time.

Grandad starts jigging to the music. Pelts moves the empty chairs back, away from the hole, and Mum starts dancing too, in her slow way—clapping behind the beat and swaying. Pelts grabs hold of Mum's forearm because she's unsteady. We've had too much grog and Mum is so skinny—she's very unsteady. We're all unsteady.

Our eyes glow like firefly sparks, our faces luminous. We pick up pace with the music, possessed with the wordless dance. We skip around the hole and the fire, waving our arms until we're sweaty and spent. We only stop because Grandad loses his footing and he nearly goes in the hole. That brings us back to the cold deadness of things. It puts an end to the dancing.

Pelts turns down the music. He tops up the drinks and the fire. We settle back to standing around the hole and I start talking.

We're not taking him out of the hole, I say. That's his resting place—it's part of his story. I want to put something here on the earth, to mark the spot, so that people can't just walk over him without even knowing.

Like a tombstone? asks Pelts.

No, I say.

Mum says: Teddy used to pick the fluffy-topped beach grass for me, lamb's-tail, bunches of it. I had it everywhere around the house. He always brought me things, mostly the lamb's-tail, but shells and driftwood and seagrasses, too. And all the little ti-tree blossoms, if it was the time for ti-tree snow, otherwise the brown-green leaves. He'd pick them up, one by one, patiently, all that tiny earth-coloured confetti. He'd bring it to me, cupped in his dear little hands, and I'd put it in bowls around the house, like offerings, as if the brown-green leaves had special powers and our luck would change. If we had the blossom we made wishes, sprinkling the papery white petals like magic dust …

Pelts throws another leafy branch on the fire.

Grandad says: It sparkles like stars, wishing stars.

Pelts says: What about a ti-tree, then, to mark the spot?

No, says Mum. Ti-trees need to be planted in groups because they're shallow-rooted. They survive because they stand in groups. They're safe in their numbers, like a family, safe in their crooked togetherness, protecting each other from the wind. They're top-heavy and without each other the wind is too much—it unearths them, uproots them.

They drop their blossom quietly, like whispering, Mum says, and their dead leaves—a breath of wind is enough to shake the deadness away and then they stand, still again, and green. The wind quietens and they go on greenly as if the dead leaving them was nothing but a breath of wind.

Their limbs are twisted, their trunks a network of veins: a plait of brown, bark veins. Mum sighs deeply: They're silly trees, shallow-rooted with spindly trunks, but they're sea trees and I love them. They're part of this place.

I had no one to stand beside me except you, Shells, and you were too small to have planted your roots firmly. Life here is planted on a sand belt. Things give way and come up from under when you least expect it, no matter how strong you are.

Teddy was strong like a good, good man and I was stronger with him and I thought I was strong enough without him. I went on greenly, for you, Shells. My roots were clawing at the sand. I was trying to keep hold, but I was unsteady. Careering down dunes. I was out of control, running away from dead things, losing my grip. I was coming undone, unplaiting myself as I ran wildly with the wind, in all directions, and there was no one to keep me upright. We're on a sand belt here and things fall through your fingers.

I did my best, Shells—it wasn't good enough for Teddy and it wasn't good enough for you. It's hard to stand beside yourself when your best isn't good enough. My best wasn't good enough to see me stand beside my children, not good enough to see us stand together and keep hold ...

If you're not together with your people, like a family, the sand life wins and the wind takes hold and you're unwrung. Then there's nothing to hold you together because you're in the sand, and that's a shaky start if you're not linked together at the roots. Then the sand wins, not that the sand cares about winning, but the sand starts to shift between your roots if you can't hold on to your people. And if the wind is

175

at you, relentlessly, you can't stand up anymore. You're not a mother if you can't stand up with your roots planted. You're just dead wood, firewood, or perhaps a home for the lizards and the spiders, or driftwood if you end up in the water. If you're lucky you end up in the wash.

In a way, I wish they'd never found Teddy and he'd stayed in the sea, but then I wouldn't have been able to do the mother-love touches and the last kisses ...

And I'm glad, Shells, that you know where he is. She sighs: We're back here, together now.

We stand together around the hole, listening to Mum. She's talking to the fire and we listen. We move to the quiet music because the moving is like words, and we hold hands and move and speak to each other in that way.

I say: It has to be a windvane, then, doesn't it, Mum? There's nothing else that would be right.

Pelts says: There used to be a windvane on the other side of the house. Near the kitchen window. But the north and south were broken and so I took it down. I could buy you another one.

A windvane, I say again. It's the right thing to put here when you think of everything together. It's the only thing to put here. We'll plant the fluffy-topped beach grass all the way around the base at the bottom: a circle of lamb's-tail around a big, round concrete base for shells and driftwood and the ti-tree blossom. *Mum?*

Perfect, Shells, she answers, words strangled and gulping.

We sway together in the wordless dance.

I feel him in the wind near the water, I say.

He was only a boy, says Pelts, crying wildly, and yet a man before his time. He put the rest of us to shame.

I say: Grandad. Do you want to say something?

Grandad looks to the trees and the water—shivering grey branches like flailing arms—silver-flecked darkness—the seductive wash—calling, calling. Grandad lifts his nose, sniffing the salty breeze greedily.

I throw another bushy head of ti-tree on the fire and watch the sparks. We turn to Grandad and wait. I take Grandad's hands in mine. *Grand?* Is there something you want to say?

Grandad looks at the hole. The mound of clay.

You've made a very big mess, he says. A shocking, muddy mess. You'll have to clean it up, you know.

Acknowledgements

Thank you to Matthew for the love, for the unfettered faith in me.

Thank you to our ace children: Albert, Amelia, Grace, Henry, Matilda and Heidi—for respecting the retreat that writing requires—for love and laughter in the everyday circus.

Thank you to my loyal friend and dad, Andrew: *Follow what you love*. Thanks to my loving and hysterical siblings: Samuel, Amy, Thomas and Josephine, and to their gorgeous children. Thanks to my mother-in-law, Janet, for her generous spirit.

Thank you to my precious ghosts, for walking with me, for your whisperings—to my beautiful mum, Ruth (dec.) for the abiding lessons in love and empathy, to my maternal grandmother, Honey (dec.)—*To thine own self be true*—and to Sarah (dec.), who seemed to know where I was headed all those years ago, like yesterday.

From the bottom of my heart, thank you to those who have gone out of their way to encourage me and support my writing—Michael Meehan, Sudesh Mishra, Dominique Hecq, Bruce Pascoe, Ann McCulloch, Paul Hetherington, Jen Webb and Donna Brien. For lending generous support to an emerging writer, I thank Bruce Pascoe, Amanda Lohrey, Jem Poster and Arnold Zable.

ACKNOWLEDGEMENTS

Thank you to Terri-ann White for believing in this story; I'm thrilled to be published by UWA Publishing.

Thank you to Alex Nahlous for insightful reading and fine editing.

Thanks to Terri-ann's team at UWAP: to Kate Pickard for astute management of the publication process; to Charlotte Guest for broad guidance and humour and to Alissa Dinallo for intuitive investment in the cover design.